THE REFLECTION
ON MOUNT VITAKI

THE FEY SERIES
(READING ORDER)

THE ORIGINAL BOOKS OF THE FEY

The Sacrifice: Book One of the Fey

The Changeling: Book Two of the Fey

The Rival: Book Three of the Fey

The Resistance: Book Four of the Fey

Victory: Book Five of the Fey

THE BLACK THRONE

The Black Queen: Book One of the Black Throne

The Black King: Book Two of the Black Throne

THE QAVNERIAN PROTECTORATE

The Reflection on Mount Vitaki: Prequel to the Qavnerian
Protectorate

The Kirilli Matter: The First Book of the Qavnerian Protectorate

Barkson's Journey: The Second Book of the Qavnerian Protectorate

(coming 2023)

ALSO BY
KRISTINE KATHRYN RUSCH

THE DIVING SERIES

Writing as Kris Nelscott

THE SMOKEY DALTON SERIES

A Dangerous Road

Smoke-Filled Rooms

Thin Walls

Stone Cribs

War at Home

Days of Rage

Street Justice

AND

Protectors

Writing as Kristine Grayson

The Charming Trilogy, Vol. 1

The Charming Trilogy, Vol. 2

The Fates Trilogy

The Daughters of Zeus Trilogy

THE REFLECTION
ON MOUNT VITAKI

PREQUEL TO THE QAVNERIAN PROTECTORATE

KRISTINE KATHRYN RUSCH

WMG
PUBLISHING

The Reflection on Mount Vitaki
Copyright © 2022 by Kristine Kathryn Rusch
Published by WMG Publishing
Cover and layout copyright © 2022 by WMG Publishing
Cover design by Allyson Longueira | WMG Publishing
Cover illustration by Echo Chernik
Background art © cappa | Depositphotos
Figure art © Ravven and © Cheshire Studios

ISBN-13 (trade paperback): 978-1-56146-833-1
ISBN-13 (hardcover): 978-1-56146-844-7

THE REFLECTION ON MOUNT VITAKI

CHAPTER
ONE

P rofessor Kyra Row Kirilli stood on the plateau outside the adobe house she had called home for the past fifteen years and shielded her eyes with her right hand. She had stared at the sheer wall of Mount Vitaki ever since she moved here as a Practical Intern, glad to be part of anything inside the Forbidden Valley.

That sheer wall had called to her from the moment she arrived. She had looked up at it, the setting sun reflecting off its smooth bluish-black surface, and had thought she saw something alive in the flare of light.

She hadn't, of course. She knew that now. But then, she had said something to her professor—Wellington Hammershield— the man who had hired her, and he had glared at her with something like shock.

One does not use one's imagination up here, he had said in that overly pompous way of his. *Imagination interferes with facts. You'd do well to remember that.*

She had never forgotten it, although she no longer agreed with it. Hammershield was old school; to suggest that imagination had a role in archeology was heresy to him.

In the years since, professors who specialized in studies of the mind—particularly the mind as it pertained to the arts—realized the importance of imagination. It was the impetus for learning, the beginning of the search for truth.

Which was why that mountain face across from her still held her captive.

And in the morning, she and her team would rappel down that sheer face to see what they could find.

Decades of work and study in the Razbitay Mountain Range had led her to this moment. Mount Vitaki was unlike any other mountain in the range.

None of the other mountains were as tall. They rose at predictable grade. Their summits were round. At lower elevations, the summits were covered in dirt and desert plants. The mountains that had peaks at the higher elevations were covered in snow much of the year.

Mount Vitaki looked like a needle rising into the air. Its peak was more of a point, not that she had seen it much. The peak was almost always covered in clouds. In all the years she had lived and worked here, the peak had been visible only a few times. She never knew what made it visible, but she imagined that a strong violent wind had pushed the clouds away for a minute or two.

When that happened, she saw the tip of the needle. The moments were brief—too quick to capture with her camera. The exposures, which took at least five minutes, were too slow. By the time the camera completed its recording of a scene, the sky had changed, the clouds returned, and Mount Vitaki's peak had disappeared into a fluffy white ring of moisture and fog.

She had sketched the peak several times, and had some of her Practical Interns do the same. That was the reason she brought artists with her to the Forbidden Valley. Artists were able to capture on canvas or on paper what the slow-moving cameras could not.

In some ways, the images created by the artists (*using their imaginations*, she always wanted to tell Hammershield who was now long-dead) were more accurate than anything the camera reported.

She let out a breath. She always knew she was nervous about something new here when she mentally argued with Hammershield. He had given her a start in the studies of the forgotten elements of the ancient world, but he had also filled her with neurosis that had yet to leave.

He would have laughed at that, saying that a professor's job was to imbue his students with both learning and a lifetime of questions.

He had done that much, at least.

She wasn't sure if she did the same for the Practical Interns she brought with her every year from Serebro Academy. Sure, she gave them a good course of study for her annual four months at the academy. But once they got here, they were glorified servants who did as she told them to do.

Many of them left and never returned. Some didn't even finish out their assigned plan to make them active archeologists.

Her husband, Magnus, believed that the number of students who left was not a problem. He often told her that teaching them what they *didn't* want to be was as important as teaching them what they did want to be.

That sounded like a platitude to her, but the academy seemed to agree. They didn't mind that she graduated fewer of her Practical Interns than any other professor in the department.

Sometimes she thought her Practical Interns quit because she did not understand people who so easily gave up on their dreams. But then, she had known from childhood that she wanted to learn all about the ancient cultures that had come from the Forbidden Valley.

Before she had Hammershield as her primary professor, she had said that discovering all there was to know about the

Forbidden Valley was her calling. Afterwards, she simply told people she had always wanted to study here.

But in her heart, the word *calling* remained. She couldn't even remember when she first learned about the valley. It had always been a part of her.

Her mother claimed she had learned about it at the Mazurka Museum. For decades, the museum prominently displayed a diorama of the Forbidden Valley.

She visited that diorama often in childhood, and later, as an adult studying the Forbidden Valley, she had visited the diorama on a break. That was when she realized that the diorama's depiction of the valley was 100 percent accurate, but its depiction of Mount Vitaki was three-quarters of a guess.

No one had ever scaled that mountain, although hundreds had tried. No one had ever been able to figure out why its eastern face was so smooth. The legends were silent, the myths non-existent.

At least about that part of Mount Vitaki. The locals had a million different stories about the mountain, none of which seemed credible to her. She didn't focus on the myths and legends like some of her colleagues, but she did look at the similarities in the stories, to find some kind of truth about this part of the Dorovich continent.

Thus far, she hadn't found a lot of truth, except about the Forbidden Valley itself. More than one culture considered the valley "forbidden" but the reasons all seemed lost to the mists of time.

Over the decades, Hammershield's students had discovered a lot of evidence that the reasons weren't lost as much as destroyed. And while that had frustrated him to the very end of his days, it had intrigued Kyra.

Something about this valley was important enough to keep it pristine, but dangerous enough to prevent anyone from actively exploring it—until the last 100 years or so, when Qavner finally extended its power over the Forbidden Valley, as part of the Qavnerian Protectorate.

The existence of the Protectorate made it easy for academics like Kyra to work and study in the valley. Travel was still difficult and communication was often a logistical nightmare, so she coped with both by informing the academy about what she was doing after she had done it.

No one there had any idea that she was bringing a team to explore the mountain. And certainly no one knew that she had paid for a demiglider to land on the peak.

Rappelling down the side scared her less than the trip to the top of Mount Vitaki on the demiglider.

Demigliders were still a new and dangerous technology. Very few people even knew how to operate a demiglider, let alone operate one in the strange wind currents around a mountain.

But she didn't want her team to climb the mountain. She wasn't even sure climbing the sheer sides of the mountain was possible. Over the generations, several others had tried it, and all of them had failed.

So demiglider it was. If she wanted to find out what caused the reflection, she would have to travel *down* to it, not climb up to it.

She had participated in dangerous climbs before, but none of them like this one.

The pilot she had hired, Zed, claimed there was a small plateau on the top. He had landed there, he said, more than once.

She worried that he had landed somewhere else, maybe even on a different mountain. She had heard that demigliders were notoriously unreliable, that they were extremely difficult to navigate. She had even heard that some pilots lost a sense of where they were once they were in the air.

She doubted she would be able to sleep tonight. If there was no plateau, all of her planning was for naught. She also fretted about the dangers of flying toward that mountain, and discovering it was not as expected.

Magnus seemed calmer about this than she was. He reminded her that if there was no plateau, the demiglider would not land. He had also reminded her that he had helped her pick the date and time of this mission, and that the numbers made it auspicious.

She trusted his numbers. Magnus had two specialties—alchemy and numerology. He understood alchemical theory better than most, but he had a gift for numerology. When he said that numbers were auspicious, he was always right.

He was convinced this mission would change both of their lives.

She let that conviction get her to this moment. She had planned every detail with Magnus's numbers in mind. She had even double-checked the birth dates and other relevant numbers with the team she had chosen. Magnus had declared that all of them would be changed by this mission.

She had even decided against using two of her regular climbing companions because their numbers did not work with hers, at least on that date and at that particular time.

She had even checked the dates for her son, who was with his grandparents for the entire summer. According to Magnus, if she rappelled the mountain tomorrow, the future of the entire Kirilli family would be different than it had been before.

That part worried her. Her death would change everyone's lives as well. But Magnus had said the date was auspicious, not dangerous. And it would be auspicious for her.

Dying was not auspicious for her.

The other reason she had chosen the day was because it had the longest window. Magnus had been very clear as she planned this mission: some of the trips she looked at would have to happen within the space of an hour. That was simply not long enough for the team to rappel down the mountain's face, and then get back up.

Tomorrow looked good all day long. Not that she would need an entire day. She needed the morning, and maybe part of the afternoon. She hoped that she wouldn't need the afternoon, though. This was a preliminary exploration, so that she would know what was ahead.

As such, she didn't want her people too tired. And she didn't want the pilot to wait too long for them. He assured her that he could handle an hours-long wait and still remain mentally clear, but she wasn't certain that was true.

She certainly didn't want to test it, particularly with something as dangerous as a demiglider.

The sun was thin this afternoon, which she did not like. The air was clear, as it usually was, and smelled faintly of dust. No rain on the breeze, which was a good thing.

But she wanted a full-on sunny day. She wanted a chance to see the reflection tonight, just before she left.

She wanted confirmation that she was doing the right thing.

Behind her, the glass door slammed. She winced. It didn't matter how many times she'd asked Magnus not to slam the glass door, he always did. Or rather, he let it close on its own, which was the same thing as slamming it.

His feet crunched softly on the dirt as he approached her. She bit back a thread of irritation. He knew that sunset was her moment with the mountain. He usually didn't encroach on it.

But she supposed, she needed to be a bit more compassionate. He had supported her all along through this project, and he didn't get to go to the mountain. He had to watch from here tomorrow. Watch, wait, and hope that everything went perfectly well.

He reached her side. The air suddenly smelled of peppermint.

He was clutching two mugs of tea.

"Thought you could use this," he said, and thrust one of the mugs at her.

She smiled at him. He found peppermint tea soothing. She just liked how it tasted. But she had never disabused him of his notion that peppermint tea soothed her as much as it soothed him.

"Thank you," she said, and wrapped both hands around the mug. It was warm, but not hot, even though the tea was steaming. The mug felt good against her skin, warming her all over.

She hadn't realized the breeze had a chill. She had been a little cold.

She glanced sideways at her husband of ten years. They had met as they were Advanced Students, even though they were in separate departments. They had overlapped in a Magic of Science seminar and Magnus had shared notes with her.

She had had trouble understanding how anyone could believe in magic. Science answered all questions, albeit slowly at times. Magnus tried to show her the ways that the inexplicable touched their lives.

He had had some success, which was why she used his numerological findings to help her make decisions. But if anyone had asked her whether or not numerology was magic, she would have said that no one had yet determined the science behind the way that it all worked.

Magnus always smiled slightly when she said that. His opinion differed. But they both respected each other's positions, especially since the positions ended in the exact same place: Neither of them knew exactly how Magnus's numerological predictions worked, but they both knew that the predictions did work.

He was staring warily at the mountain. His face had filled out since their student days, and his skin had become elastic. He was softer now, a little doughy. He looked like the professor he had become. There were laugh lines alongside his dark eyes, and a little silver in his black hair.

She always wanted to touch his ears, which were delicate, and ended in a slight point. At least their son had inherited those ears, instead of hers, which she kept covered. Hers looked like gigantic triangles affixed to the sides of her head. They were one of her few features that she actively loathed.

The sun had finally reached the edge of the mountain range. She gripped the mug hard, then made her hands relax. She didn't want to break it, and get tea all over herself.

"Any moment now," she said to him.

Magnus nodded, his mouth a thin line. He had never seen the reflection, but he had never stopped trying. He had taken its existence on faith all of these years, although she had a hunch that about five years ago he had been about to give up, when one of her Practical Interns truly saw the reflection as well.

Several of her Practical Interns had lied about seeing it, and she had always caught them in the lie. But that student, Evgenia Svirid, had just arrived in the Razbitay Mountains. She had joined the annual first day feast, and walked out of the glass doors at sunset, raising a hand in startlement.

"What the heck is that?" she had asked as she turned away.

That was the mistake all of the other Practical Interns had made. The first sighting of the reflection was often painful and blinding.

Even now, after years, Kyra sometimes had to look down or put out a hand to block the worst of the rays.

Now, Kyra looked away from Magnus and back at the mountain. She thought she saw a glimmer, like a bit of glass catching the sun, but nothing more.

Her heart sank. Today of all days, she needed to see the reflection. She needed a reminder that what she was doing was right.

Then light flared—blue and red and gold and green, alternating like as if someone was turning a crystal in their hands. The light was so intense it brought tears to her eyes.

"Do you see it?" she asked, hoping that this time, with the reflection so very bright, that Magnus would finally catch the glimmer.

"No." The word was flat. She would have thought it devoid of emotion, except that she knew him almost better than she knew herself. He was disappointed.

She had two emotional reactions at the same time: she was disappointed that he couldn't see this, but elated that she could.

It was almost as if the mountain had given her a gift, almost as if the mountain was beckoning to her, almost as if the mountain wanted her to discover its secrets.

She never told anyone that she felt like that. It was too close to Magnus's "magic is everywhere" malarky. Magic wasn't everywhere. Magic didn't exist.

This was some kind of science, a reflection, maybe of something major, something so large that she and her team would see it when they hit that point on the mountain where the reflection originated.

The sun dipped behind the mountain range, coloring the handful of wispy clouds around the tops of the other mountains red and gold. But the reflection hadn't faded as the sun did.

Instead, the reflection turned a bright whitish gold. The light enveloped her and held her. She had no idea how Magnus could not see this. It felt like she was bathed in light.

Then the glow faded. Her breath caught.

The mountain had blessed her.

She turned toward Magnus, and he tilted his head toward her, his eyes sad.

"You saw it," he said.

"It was incredible," she said.

"I'm glad," he said and took a sip of his tea. Slurped it really, maybe because he knew that annoyed her.

Then he raised the mug toward her in an obvious toast.

"To tomorrow," he said.

She raised her mug and clinked his. "To tomorrow, and all the changes it will bring."

"May they be good ones," he said, sounding wistful.

She felt that thread of irritation again. He had said that they would be good. He had said the numbers promised that.

"Yes," she said, not letting the irritation out. "May they all be for the very best."

TWO

Dawn broke through a thin layer of clouds that streaked the sky like ribbons. Kyra wore a wool sweater over her climbing gear, her arms tucked under her armpits for warmth.

The wind was slight, but icy. The day would heat up as the sun rose high in the sky, but right now, it felt like the earliest days of winter, even though it was high summer. The mountains were always colder than the valley, but she was not usually up early enough to feel that chill.

She wasn't the only one trying to keep herself warm. Alyoshi, the oldest on the team, was actually stomping his feet, his hands in the pocket of a great coat he would have to leave behind. Fortunately, he had brought a duffel that they could lock in the single outbuilding near the runway.

Alyoshi was a big man, almost too large to be an effective climber, and yet somehow he managed. Like Kyra, he was a professor at Serebro Academy. Unlike Kyra, he only spent summers in the mountains, preferring the academic life through the rest of the year.

Normally, she wouldn't have climbed with Alyoshi. She

preferred his advice on all things from the Forbidden Valley—the myths and legends of this place were his specialty. He was a good climber and often led a group of students on sightseeing climbs throughout the Razbitay range. But he had ceased doing adventure climbing a few years ago.

However, from the beginning of Kyra's work here, Alyoshi had asked to accompany her when (if) she climbed Mount Vitaki. She had quietly discouraged him, until this trip.

Then she had asked him if he considered rappelling down the side climbing, and he had grinned at her, his mouth nearly lost in his bushy black beard.

Yes, he had said. *Yes, of course.*

Even if it means flying in a demiglider? She had asked, since that had been a sticking point for a few others.

Even if, he had replied with a wave of the hand. Apparently, the demiglider didn't bother him.

It bothered the others. Uliana, a tall blond professional climber from the Forbidden Valley, had quietly protested the demiglider when Kyra had asked her to accompany them.

I would prefer to climb up, Uliana had said, hands clasped primly behind her.

I would too, Kyra had replied, *but every time I've tried, the mountain would not give me purchase.*

Uliana had smiled ever so faintly at that. *We have had the same problem.*

We referred to her and her partner Matvei. Matvei was the one with ties to Serebro. He was an unaffiliated Scholar, with as many degrees as Kyra had, but he chose not to use them to teach. Either he had private money or he and Uliana made more from their tourist climbs than Kyra would have guessed.

He spent his time here in the mountains researching all sorts of things that Kyra had never asked about. He claimed to have a book nearly finished, but as long as she had known him, he had said that the book was "nearly" done.

Matvei was wiry and strong, a quick thinker who enhanced every climb she'd accompanied him on. He was the prickly center of the climbing community in this part of the mountains, and she was happy he had agreed to join her.

She needed this trip to be a success.

The only part of the mission he disapproved of was the demiglider. He was the only one of the four climbers who had never taken a test flight in the demiglider, and refused to ask how the demiglider worked. He almost decided not to accompany her, because they were flying up to the peak on the demiglider itself.

Kyra understood his hesitation. She wasn't fond of the demiglider either. She'd been in it twice before, the second time flying near Mount Vitaki. The demiglider was safe enough, or so the pilot, Zed, had assured her. He had installed a number of safety features that would, he said, keep them all alive.

She didn't like to think about vehicles that needed safety features to keep everyone alive, and had said so to Zed. He had smiled at her.

Pilots are daredevils, he had said. *We like to push the limits of our crafts. Sometimes those limits are very dangerous.*

How dangerous? she had asked him.

I used to fly without air masks, he had said, his black eyes twinkling, *until the day I took the demiglider so high that I blacked out. Fortunately, I woke up when the demiglider went into its dive, and I was able to correct. I've known a few other pilots who weren't as lucky.*

She had nearly canceled the trip right then and there, but he had assured her that he had been "a long ways" above the peak of Mount Vitaki when the blackout occurred.

He'd scouted the top of the mountain for her twice before saying it was safe for her and her team to travel there. He claimed that the top of the mountain was flat, not the point that it seemed to be. He did worry that it was usually enshrouded in clouds—but he wasn't worried for himself or the demiglider, but for the trip the four of them were going to take down the side of the mountain.

He knew enough about climbing to know that weather always had an impact on climbers.

Zed had been checking and double-checking all the parts of the demiglider since Kyra arrived.

The demiglider was shaped like a bird with its wings extended. It had three wheels, two beneath the wings, and one beneath the front compartment where Zed would sit alone.

The bottom of the demiglider contained all of the moving parts, which he had tried to show her more than once. The windstone tubes that gave him control over the demiglider, the vents that opened and closed according to some work he could do inside his area—which he called a cockpit. There were gears and levers and all kinds of dials in that cockpit, which told Zed things about the demiglider that he wanted to explain to her, but she refused to listen.

She didn't have to fly the demiglider; she just had to trust that it would work as it needed to. Her stomach flopped at the thought. Maybe she was more like Matvei than she thought.

The fact that this was her third trip in a demiglider did not make the trip any easier. If anything, it became harder.

Zed ran a hand along one side of the demiglider, as if he was petting it. Then he turned around.

"We're ready," he said.

That was a large assumption. He was ready. Or he and the demiglider were ready. Kyra wasn't ready. She wasn't sure she would ever be.

She bit back questions that rose in her mind. They only came up because she was nervous. She would be double-checking or maybe triple-checking what he had already told her.

The team was within the weight limits that he had set. The equipment fell into those requirements as well. Zed had already taken a bit of their equipment to the mountaintop a few days ago and set everything up.

She had to trust him, and she had to be confident for her team.

She smiled at him, and walked toward the demiglider, hoping the others would follow.

The wind seemed stronger than it had a few minutes ago, but that was probably her imagination as well. The wind was always a factor here.

They were on a plateau on one of the ridges across the Hidden River from Mount Vitaki. The plateau was the highest and broadest unsettled ridge in the Razbitay Mountain Range.

Zed had told her that he needed a lot of area to build up speed before the demiglider went off the side of the ridge. The demiglider would have to climb to Mount Vitaki's peak, which was always work for the demiglider.

In the early days of demigliding, the demigliders only went down—unless they caught an air current. Nowadays, the windstone tubes and vents ensured that a demiglider could go up or down according to the will of the pilot.

She didn't turn around to see if the others were following. Instead, she focused on the demiglider itself. It had four bubbleglass compartments. The cockpit, with its smaller bubbleglass top; the second compartment with a bench seat that fit at least two; the third compartment which was just over the wings, also seating two; and the fourth compartment with just a bit of bubbleglass for either a small passenger or, as in this instance, a place to put equipment.

Kyra walked around the side of the demiglider, always stunned at how long and tall the demiglider was. It looked smaller from a distance, maybe because of its bird-like shape. Up close, though, it was taller than she was—taller than Alyoshi in some parts.

There were steps that allowed her to climb into the

demiglider. They were carved into the side and had to be covered before the demiglider started its journey. She was sharing the second compartment with Alyoshi, partly because it was the largest compartment, and he was not small. Technically, maybe, Uliana should have been beside him, but Kyra wanted to be as close to Zed and that cockpit as possible.

Matvei and Uliana had to climb on a strut, then cross the wing—very carefully so that they didn't damage it—in order to climb into their compartment.

They all set their equipment on the ground behind the demiglider. Zed would put the equipment away, not the team. He had to distribute the weight just so.

Kyra put her gloved hands on the side of the demiglider. The stone was so cold that she could feel the chill through her gloves. The wind seemed stronger on the side of the demiglider, or maybe on this side of the plateau.

She paused as she climbed and peered across the plateau at Mount Vitaki itself.

They were just below the circular layer of clouds. Technically, she supposed, they were across from the reflection point, but she couldn't see it, not from here.

In fact, from here, that section of Mount Vitaki, about a third of the way down from the peak, looked like black, as if an intensely dark shadow had blocked out all light altogether.

She shivered, and made herself climb in. Then she slid across so that Alyoshi didn't have to climb over her as he got into the demiglider.

The bubbleglass on the cockpit was up, so that Zed could climb in. Kyra stared at the stick which controlled much of the motion of the demiglider. The stick didn't look sturdy at all. It was long and thin, and it looked like something that could snap off in Zed's fingers if he twisted it too hard.

She couldn't read the dials. They were on the board in front of the stick, six different dials, perfectly round with some kind of moving arrow inside of each one. Zed had tried to explain their purpose to her on her first flight and she had finally told him that he was only confusing her. She didn't want to know the details of flying this thing.

The vague overview he had given her at the start had been unnerving enough.

Alyoshi pulled himself into the second compartment and sat down heavily, rocking the demiglider as he did so. Behind her, Kyra could hear footsteps on the wings, and she wondered if Zed had told Uliana and Matvei to be careful as they climbed.

He probably had. Zed was nothing if not careful.

Kyra took a deep breath, trying to make her heartbeat slow down. She didn't want the team to know how very nervous she was.

"Ready?" Alyoshi asked her with a grin. The grin made his eyes light up, and she was stunned to realize that he was actually looking forward to this part of the trip.

She nodded, trying to sound enthusiastic. "I've wanted to do this for years."

Then Alyoshi gave her a knowing glance. "But not the demiglider part."

"Does anyone like doing the demiglider part?" she asked lightly.

"I don't mind it," he said. Then he tilted his head backwards, at the third section. "But they do."

She looked over her shoulder. Uliana and Matvei were settling into their seats. Zed had already put their bubbleglass down over the compartment.

They looked nervous, something Kyra wasn't used to seeing from them.

Zed had put down the bubbleglass for the back compartment as well, which meant that the equipment was on board. For some reason, that calmed her.

As if he heard her thoughts, Zed peered into their compartment.

"Ready?" he asked.

The question was starting to annoy her. But she smiled at him, and nodded.

"Get your hands free," he said to Alyoshi, who had rested one hand on the side of the compartment.

Alyoshi moved his hand quickly as if he hadn't realized he'd been holding that part of the demiglider.

"You know where the air masks are, right?" Zed asked.

Both Alyoshi and Kyra nodded.

"I'm going to want you to use them," Zed said. "Everyone reacts differently when the demiglider travels as high as that peak, and I want to make sure the four of you are all right."

"Okay," Kyra said, not liking the way her stomach flipped at the thought. She wasn't sure what he meant by different reactions, and she wasn't going to ask for clarification. But she could guess.

Zed had said he had passed out once when he traveled too high. He didn't want any of them to do so.

She fumbled for the air mask compartment underneath the seat. She had no idea how the air masks worked, but she knew that they did. They provided fresh air that wasn't part of the air inside the compartment.

The mask scratched against her fingers, but she put it on with no troubles. The air it fed into her nose was slightly cooler than the air in the compartment.

Alyoshi was wearing his mask as well, tugging at the side straps. With his wild hair and beard, he looked like some kind of outdoor creature, with a very large snout.

Kyra turned once again toward Uliana and Matvei, preparing to gesture at them to make sure they were wearing their air masks. But this time, when she looked at them, they had the masks on.

She nodded at them, smiling, even though they couldn't see the smile. She turned back around in her seat just in time to see Zed clamber into his compartment, carefully moving his legs around the stick, checking the dials before he did anything else. Then he grasped a handle inside his bubbleglass cover, and pulled it down over the compartment.

Now, they couldn't really converse with each other. There was an emergency communications device, but she had learned on a previous flight that it only broadcast in one direction.

Zed could give them all commands from the cockpit, but they could not communicate with him, not even if they were in some kind of trouble.

Zed touched the dials, and did something with his left hand that she couldn't quite see. The demiglider vibrated which she now knew—after her flights—meant that the windstone tubes had been activated.

Zed explained enough to her that she knew the tubes sucked air inside just before the demiglider moved forward. Then the tubes would propel the air out of the bottom vents, making the demiglider rise off the ground.

From there it was all wind patterns and movements of that stick, things that sounded way too technical for her.

The vibrations would end once the demiglider had no ground underneath it at all. She wasn't sure how she felt about the vibrations; she hated the way they made her teeth rattle, but she also hated moving away from the ground entirely.

The demiglider eased forward and then, suddenly, the vibrations eased. Zed moved the stick easily, and he seemed to have settled back in his seat.

Kyra hadn't. She had one hand braced against the front of the compartment, the other clinging the seat edge below.

She stared straight ahead. On her first trip, she had looked down, and that had made her physically ill. It had been all she could do to keep her food down.

She knew she was far in the air. She just didn't want to think about it.

Alyoshi was staring straight ahead as well. If she hadn't known him so well, she would have thought him less terrified than she was. At least he wasn't clinging to the bottom of his seat with one hand.

But the other hand was braced against the front of the compartment just like her hand was. Only his fingers were bent, digging into the side as if he could carve finger-sized holes in it.

Beyond him, she could see the northern part of the Forbidden Valley—the Razbitay Mountain Range rising on both sides, the mountains looking like jagged teeth disappearing into the distance.

In the time it had taken them to get off the plateau, the sun had come all the way up. Its light looked thin, though, almost tentative. The sky was blue, but tinged with gray. Clouds had formed around the demiglider—or, as Zed had warned—it was actually approaching the clouds.

That was one of the things that made her the most nervous —the clouds around that peak. Zed had said that flying into clouds was not a problem, but Kyra had never experienced it.

There were a lot of firsts on this trip, all of which made her nervous.

She hated to go into any kind of mission as a bundle of nerves, but there was no way around it this time.

And she really had no one to confide in about the trip either. She hadn't wanted to upset Magnus; he was worried enough. And she had to be strong for her team.

She probably could have confided in Zed, but she really hadn't known him long enough to feel comfortable with that.

Rain speckled the windglass. Fluffy grayness surrounded the demiglider. Her breath caught. Zed had warned them all that this would happen when they went inside a cloud, but she still hadn't expected it.

It felt like she had gone from a beautiful sunny morning into an approaching storm.

Through the windglass, Kyra could see Zed. His right hand was on the stick. In front of him, the arrows on the dials bounced. Below those dials were tiny levers that Zed had explained to her once.

The levers controlled the vents in the windstone tube. Right now, Zed was manipulating them. His hands were moving faster than she thought humanly possible. He kept his gaze on the windglass before him, apparently monitoring all three sides.

He needed to. The demiglider was rising upwards and now Kyra couldn't see anything except gray and water on the windglass. The rain droplets had gotten really big and ice was threaded through them. Wind howled around the demiglider, rocking it. Or maybe the demiglider rocked like this normally. She didn't really know.

She had no idea how Zed was seeing anything, but he didn't seem panicked, at least from behind. His movements, with that stick and occasionally waving a hand over those dials, seemed calm and assured.

Kyra glanced at Alyoshi. His face had gone pale and his eyes were wide. His arm was extended straight, as if he was no longer bracing himself, but trying to push himself all the way back into the wooden seat. His blue eyes flicked to the windglass surrounding them, as if the weather scared him or as if he thought the glass would break.

Kyra looked away. She didn't want to know how terrified Alyoshi was. Or anyone else on the team for that matter.

She was having enough trouble dealing with herself.

The demiglider rose and dropped and rose some more. Zed had warned her that would happen.

Air currents are fickle things, he'd said, *and we're tampering with them. So make sure you're prepared for some difficulties.*

Preparing for some difficulties and experiencing them were

two different things. She didn't like the way that the adrenaline was coursing through her.

She had to calm down or she would have some kind of physical crash before she even started. She had brought food—they all had, because they did not know how long it would take them to get down to the reflection point—or back up, for that matter.

But that wasn't the same as figuring out a way to cope with full physical exhaustion.

The speaker in front of her crackled so loudly that Kyra looked up at first, thinking the windglass had finally shattered. Alyoshi looked up too, his eyes wild.

Even if she kept herself reasonably calm (and she wasn't), her team was going to be frazzled.

That was one thing she hadn't planned for—among many, apparently.

The speaker crackled again, even louder this time. Then Zed's voice came through, tinny and flat, without some of the warmth that made him sound like Zed.

"We're coming in low. Brace yourselves."

Whatever that meant. Her heartbeat sped up, and she was having trouble breathing. Her ice-cold fingers, trapped inside the glove, could no longer gain purchase under the seat, so she let go, nearly causing herself to lose her balance.

She put the hand on the seat, keeping the other hand braced like it had been.

The wooden seat was cold, so cold that she could feel it through her glove. She hadn't realized when it had gotten this cold, and that concerned her. She wasn't usually this oblivious.

She wasn't usually this frightened.

The clouds up front got thicker. She had no idea how Zed knew they were coming in low, whatever that meant.

And then, the demiglider slammed down on something hard, bounced, and rose slightly.

Now, Zed's movements were frantic. He was working that

stick with both hands and one knee. The other knee was pressed against the front of the cockpit as if he could use his leg to control something as well.

Maybe he could. She didn't know.

The demiglider hit the ground (or whatever it was) again, and then rose again. It went down, harder this time, and sped forward, going so fast that the water against the windglass ran in horizontal streaks.

She thought she heard a scream, but that couldn't be possible, right? The windglass hadn't allowed the five of them to communicate before now, so how could she hear anything from behind her?

Alyoshi was biting his lower lip so hard that he had drawn blood. His eyes met hers, fearful and begging—but for what, she didn't know. For it all to stop? That didn't seem like Alyoshi. He was usually one of the stronger people she climbed with.

She could rely on him. That was one reason he was here.

Zed was doing something with his feet. The demiglider wasn't going as fast. He pushed forward on that stick.

The wheels beneath the demiglider squealed and groaned. The entire demiglider shook, not like it had before in the wind, but like it was going to come apart from the effort of trying to stop.

It suddenly turned sideways and skidded, the wind pushing it, or so it seemed. Apparently Zed thought the same thing because he moved just one hand away from that stick, and punched the wind vents, closing them? Opening them? She didn't know and couldn't ask and wasn't sure if she wanted to anyway.

The demiglider finally screeched to a stop, then wobbled like it was shivering with terror all on its own.

No one moved. It was as if they all couldn't believe they had arrived here.

Wherever here was. She couldn't see out the windglass at all.

The rain continued to pummel the glass, and the wind kept shaking the demiglider.

She hadn't planned on weather like this, although Zed had told her that the clouds brought weather to the mountain's peak. She hadn't thought it would be much of an issue. He hadn't told her that the clouds brought *storms*, only rain and cold and the occasional bit of wind.

Disappointment welled in her. All she wanted to do was *see* this place, and now, even though she was here, she couldn't even do that.

Zed hadn't moved either. He gripped that stick, his head down ever so slightly as if he was looking at something on the control panel in front of him. She couldn't ask him what it was.

Or what they were going to do next.

She knew what she wanted to do. She wanted to leave, but she wasn't sure they could. They couldn't see anything, except gray.

She mentally shook a fist at the clouds and rain and storm around her. All she wanted to do was see that reflection point.

All she wanted to do was what it had always felt like she was meant to do.

She let out a small breath, and willed her heart rate to slow.

And as she did, the clouds parted all around her, almost as if they were retreating.

Sunlight poured down on the windglass. Water dripped off it, and the little bits of ice melted. The light seemed to come down on her, not on Alyoshi.

The sunlight almost felt like an answer to her prayers—not that she was the praying type. She felt about religion the way her father felt about magic—as if it were something to be banished and destroyed.

She shook off the thought, and stared at the world around her. First at the clouds, which were backing off horizontally in a circle, as if the sunlight had burned a hole in them and chased them away.

The top of Mount Vitaki revealed itself slowly. First, the area around the demiglider appeared, red and brown and incredibly flat. The rain had turned the ground into something like mud, only it wasn't deep enough to be mud. Wet sand, almost, or some other material, one she didn't entirely recognize.

It took her a moment to realize that the clouds had backed off all the way to the edge of the mountain peak. There were no trees here, no growth at all, just a flat area as if someone had used a knife to carve off the top of the mountain itself.

She hadn't expected that. She had expected the top of the mountain to be a point, even though Zed had told her that it wasn't. He had said it was flat, and that there was a good landing area, but apparently a large part of her didn't accept it.

From the time she was very little, she thought of the top of Mount Vitaki as the point of a needle. Maybe in the back of her mind, she had seen the demiglider balanced on the top of that point, the glider's center rocking back and forth as if it were rocking on the head of a pin.

Of course that wasn't what was here. Of course, or Zed wouldn't have flown them here. He had said there was enough room. He had said the top of Mount Vitaki was sturdy enough for them to use it as a base for going down the mountainside.

The light sprawled out more, revealing the edges of the mountain top. It was wide and long. The demiglider could have gone farther without toppling off the edge.

The only thing here, though, besides the demiglider, were tracks from the other times that Zed had landed. And maybe a few footprints, although she wasn't sure if that was her eyes playing tricks.

The sunlight seemed like late afternoon sunlight, even though it was still early morning. She knew about that, though.

They were incredibly high up, and the thinner the air, the brighter and more powerful the sunlight.

Her team hadn't been this high before—and neither had she —but they hadn't started from ground level either. Still, she could feel that lightheadedness that sometimes came from higher elevations.

She needed some liquid and something sweet to calm her entire system.

Zed finally turned in his seat and faced her. He raised his eyebrows, making his long face seem comically long. He was asking her if she still wanted to do this.

She actually wasn't certain. That storm had scared her and if it returned, getting off this peak might be hard. What she really wanted to do was talk to him.

She pointed at the windglass bubble, hoping he understood. He smiled just a little and nodded, then reached behind his seat and activated the lever that raised his windglass bubble.

It slowly rode up, the water dripping off the sides, and a little bit into the cockpit.

Then he pulled the lever to raise the bubble covering Kyra and Alyoshi. The air flew in, ice-cold and with an edge of moisture coating the surface, yet it felt almost dry.

Kyra shivered, anxious to get moving. She knew better than to get out immediately, though. She waited until Zed released the bubble on the two remaining team members behind her.

Once that bubble creaked upward, Kyra took off her air mask. Then she pulled herself upward with just her legs. She put her hands on the side of the bubble, levered herself over the edge, and did her best not to sit on it, so she wouldn't get wet. She managed to fall/slide off the side and land on her feet.

The cold instantly pulled at her brow and poked at her eyes. The wind up here was stronger than she expected.

But the air smelled crisp and fresh, close to perfect.

Her heart lifted, although she wasn't sure if that was the altitude. Her mood lifted with it. She almost felt like she belonged here, like this was the perfect place to be.

Above her, the sky was blue, the sun was brilliant, and the ground hard, brown, and almost pretty. She was going to walk to the edge to look down at the reflection when she caught herself.

She needed to see to the team. She needed liquid and something sweet. She needed to get to the equipment.

She needed to check in with Zed.

She turned.

Alyoshi was levering himself out of the bubble, that terrified look still on his face. He looked even more frightened now that he was not wearing his air mask.

She hoped he wasn't frightened, not just for him and for his health, but also for the trip down the mountain's face. She still wanted to go—or maybe it was more accurate to say that she wanted to go now more than ever.

She couldn't wait to climb down, to see what was there.

Matvei was pulling a hat over his ears, which made his face hard to see. His mask was gone, but still, only his eyes were visible, and they looked like sharp black rocks glistening at her.

She could sense his reluctance to get out of the demiglider from here, but she wasn't sure if she was making that up. She turned slightly away from him, and heard a thud through the whistle of the wind.

Uliana had gotten down. She patted her thick hair to make sure that the bun on the top of her head held. She had left her air mask behind. It didn't work away from the demiglider anyway.

When her gaze met Kyra's, Uliana smiled. Her eyes crinkled and she looked as joyful as Kyra felt.

"We made it," Kyra said.

"We've only just begun this journey." That was Matvei. He sounded as sour as he looked. "We've got all day and maybe more."

"I wouldn't want to camp up here," Alyoshi said. "We're too exposed."

Kyra looked around. He was right: the top of this mountain, flat and large as it was, had no wind breaks whatsoever. That was probably why the demiglider was pushed in every direction.

Uliana held out honey water packets. She had made them before the team left. Kyra took hers gratefully, and sucked on the edge.

She needed the wet sweetness. It revived her already.

"It's always windy up here," Zed said. He had pulled the first two bubbles back over the interiors of the demiglider. He waited, somewhat impatiently, next to Matvei, who didn't seem to be putting up much of an effort to get out of the demiglider.

"Where would we be setting up?" Uliana asked. She didn't seem to care that her climbing partner was having trouble getting out of the demiglider.

She handed a packet to Alyoshi, who frowned at her.

"To sleep?" Alyoshi said. "Nowhere, I hope."

"To climb," Uliana said, in that tone people sometimes used when they were answering a particularly dumb question.

"We're not climbing," Alyoshi said, clearly bristling at her tone. "We're rappelling—"

"Maybe," Kyra said, even though just uttering the word broke her heart. "If we can't stop fighting, we're not going to do anything."

Alyoshi leaned his head back just a little, as if she had physically rebuked him.

Matvei put his head down, so that no one could see those glittery black eyes. Uliana waved a packet at him, which he took begrudgingly.

Zed looked at Kyra, eyebrows raised. She rarely spoke like that to her colleagues. To her Practical Interns, sometimes, and to unruly students in her class, always. But colleagues, never. She had even lectured Zed once on the need for respect.

But here, Matvei and Alyoshi didn't seem to respect her or the mission at all. Then Kyra smiled to herself. She kept calling this a mission, instead of a trip. Or a journey, to use Alyoshi's word.

Maybe because that was how it felt to her, like a mission she'd wanted to do her entire life.

Uliana finished her own packet, and then put the empty packet in a bag, which she held out to the others. Kyra put her own packet in the bag. Alyoshi did as well.

Uliana shook the bag at Matvei, who drank from his packet, and then tossed it in. Uliana placed the bag on the floor of the demiglider, then turned to Kyra.

"Well?" Uliana asked, as if they were continuing a conversation. Maybe they were. Kyra was having trouble keeping track. "Where are we going to set up?"

"Give me a minute." That was Zed. He had scoped out the entire top of the mountain range, which was probably why he felt he needed to answer this.

Kyra didn't want to wait for Matvei. Nor did she want to wait to pull the equipment out of the last little bubble section of the demiglider, near the tail.

She wanted to explore.

She couldn't remember a time when she had felt this restless, especially at the start of a climb.

Her brain emphasized the word *climb*, and she wanted to push it at Matvei, as almost a I-told-you-so. Any kind of adventure on the mountain, going up or down, was a climb as far as she was concerned.

And then she caught herself again.

Her emotional energy was all over the place. She was joyful, then annoyed, then almost angry underneath, impatient, and restless. That had to be the altitude, messing with her.

She had heard about this at certain elevations, but she had never experienced it before. It was almost like she was trying to catch an uncomfortable feeling she had in the pit of her stomach and label it—joy, anger, restlessness.

Instead, she needed to bottle it, and pull it out as she went down the side of the mountain.

If she went down.

"We go this way," Kyra said, as if she had been on this mountaintop before. Uliana looked at her in surprise. It was hard to get bearings on a mountaintop with no landmarks—especially one that was taller than the other mountains around it.

Besides, the clouds still hovering around the edges of the peak made this seem like it was the only place in the entire world. Kyra couldn't even see the other mountains, let alone the valley or what lay beyond them.

But Kyra didn't have to see. She knew where she was, with as much certainty as she knew her own name.

She knew how far it was to the reflection point. She knew exactly where the reflection point was, which meant she knew what side of the peak it was on, even though her own experienced team was completely turned around.

She headed toward that side of the mountaintop. Zed called her name, but she ignored him.

Out of the corner of her eye, she saw Uliana glance toward him, as if wondering what he wanted. But Kyra wasn't interested in them.

She wanted to see exactly what they all faced.

The closer she got to the edge, the more the wind slacked off. It should have remained powerful. It should have been a force she fought as she walked, but it wasn't.

This edge was unlike any other peak she had ever been on, and she had been on a lot of them.

She got close to the edge. The ground here looked like reddish-brown dirt, loose and with the consistency of sand.

Rather than stand on the edge, she got on her hands and knees, and then sprawled forward. She had no idea what was beneath her, and she didn't want her weight to strain some kind of lip. Nor did she want this sand-like dirt to crumble beneath her, and start some kind of dirt slide.

The ground beneath her was damp, but not wet, surprising, given the quality of the rain she had seen on the demiglider. The dirt was ice-cold, but not frozen, because it moved easily beneath her.

A little too easily, which made her nervous. Since they didn't have anything solid—no rocks jutting up, no thick trees, no formation of any kind, there wasn't much to tie onto.

If she wanted to rappel down, she would have to dig bolts into this dirt, far enough away for them to hold.

She crawled to the edge, dug her toes in deep, and peered over.

The side of the mountain was smooth, almost like it was made out of glass. There were no handholds, no indents in the rock face, nothing that looked like places to start and stop.

If anything, the mountainside looked like it was made out of glass, or the same kind of smooth-filed bone that needles were created out of.

The replica of Mount Vitaki that had been in the diorama that she visited over and over again in her childhood had been accurate, which sent a chill down her.

If Zed had been the first person to bring a demiglider up here, and the records did not show that anyone had managed to climb up Mount Vitaki (despite years of trying), then she did not know how that diorama had been so accurate.

And then she reminded herself that it hadn't been accurate at all. The top of the replica had been a point, like the point of a needle, not this wide flat area.

Whoever had made that replica had seen parts of Mount Vitaki, but had never made it to the top.

"You're being reckless." That was Alyoshi, behind her. "I was tempted to grab your ankles and hold you, but I was afraid that would startle you and propel you forward, given the position of your toes."

She smiled, but did not turn around.

"The surface on the sides is smooth," she said.

"What?" he asked.

Apparently, given the way the wind currents were working up here, she could hear him, but he couldn't hear her.

She almost turned and braced herself on her elbow, then thought the better of it.

Instead, she inched herself backwards, careful to stay in the footprint that she had created from her body. When she reached the place where she had last stood, she slowly rose.

Alyoshi had wisely backed out of her way. Neither of them were certain about the weight, even now.

She wiped the dirt off her front and said, "It's smooth. The side of Mount Vitaki. There are no handholds. This thing looks more like a brownish-black icicle than a mountainside."

"Maybe it is ice," he said. If it was, it would be even more unstable.

She shook her head. "It's not ice. If it was ice, it would look different. Besides, the ground up here isn't frozen, so how would ice on the sides of the mountain sustain itself?"

Even as she asked that, she wondered, though. She had no idea if that was true, because she'd never seen a mountain made out of ice before.

This one couldn't be all ice either. She'd been to the base of Mount Vitaki many times, and peered upwards into the fog and clouds, wondering what she would see. There, the mountain was wider, and had broken parts, like most mountains did. But it did have an unusual smoothness, even down there.

And that smoothness was not ice.

The dirt fell off her as she slapped her gloves against herself. The air seemed even colder than it had a moment ago, but the terrified look had left Alyoshi's face.

34

"I don't like this," he said.

She almost asked why, since she liked so much here. It wasn't like the two of them to be out of sync at all.

But she didn't. She knew why. He didn't like the strange cloud-based weather, the lack of handholds, the smooth side, the fact that the team couldn't use their usual setup. He saw only work.

She saw only opportunity.

"Zed had told us we would need bolts," she said. "He set up a few for us, remember?"

He had told them about the lack of handholds on his second trip. Kyra had asked him to set up the bolts, deep into the dirt, so that her team could rappel down using a pulley system.

Alyoshi didn't like pulleys, but he had known about it from the beginning. Maybe he had hoped for something different.

"I prefer to set up my own system," he said. "We don't even know if this ground is safe."

She slapped her gloves together getting the rest of the dirt off them. Then she made herself take a deep breath.

She usually wasn't reckless or impulsive, but this morning she wanted to throw all the plans aside and just get down that mountain.

But Alyoshi was right. Even though she had trained Zed in how to plant the bolts, he wasn't experienced, and he didn't know enough about ground cover to choose the right place.

She sighed. She wasn't going to lose this opportunity, though.

She walked over to the demiglider. Matvei had finally emerged, but he looked as nervous as Alyoshi.

Kyra had to trust her team. She had to listen to them, and not be overly excited.

On the other hand, they had already taken a huge risk by bringing an at-capacity demiglider up here. They had to take advantage of the moment.

She walked over to Zed. He seemed irritated, which she didn't blame him for, given how much trouble he was having with her team.

Trouble she hadn't prepped him for, since it was trouble she was unprepared for as well.

"Thanks for getting us up here so safely," she said.

"I'm not sure how safe it was," he said, glancing at the demiglider. It was sideways along the tracks from the previous trips. Apparently, this one hadn't gone as well as the others had.

"We're here," she said, then paused, so she didn't sound too anxious. "Could you show me where you put the bolts?"

He frowned, then closed his eyes. "I didn't, Kyra."

"What?" She felt the shock all the way to her toes.

"There was no good place to put them here, not if we wanted enough room to land the demiglider and not damage its wheels. I left the bolts over there." He pointed toward the opposite side of the peak from the reflection point.

She looked over her shoulder, feeling stunned. She hadn't expected this. She had no idea why he hadn't told her.

And it wasn't until she looked that she realized she hadn't even seen them when the demiglider landed. They were made of reinforced wood from the lower elevations of the Forbidden Valley. The wood was lacquered and strengthened. It would have been perfect had Zed inserted the bolts when he had received them.

But they'd been on this mountaintop for weeks now, subject to that weather. There would be breaking points somewhere in the middle, where the wood wasn't as firmly reinforced.

Those bolts were made specifically to hold climbers. And even more specifically to have half or more of their wood underground. That lower half was reinforced against bugs and dampness, the kinds of problems found underneath the ground, but the lower part wasn't set up to deal with unrelenting weather.

She glanced at Alyoshi, who was watching closely. She didn't know how to hide her emotions, so her disappointment was probably all over her face.

Uliana confirmed that as she sauntered over. She turned slightly, as if excluding Zed from the entire conversation.

"The bolts were never planted, huh?" she asked, and there was judgement in the tone.

"Hey," Zed said. "I pilot. I don't—"

Kyra held up a hand. She didn't care about the excuses, but she did worry that he hadn't told her. What other difficult information had he failed to impart?

"We can still use them," Uliana said.

Kyra shook her head. "They've been exposed to the elements too long."

"But they're designed to handle the weight of a team of four, right?" Uliana asked.

"Yes, but—"

"We do a combo," Uliana said. "We send two down to the reflection point, just to see what it is. No exploration. And the other two—and our *pilot* here—" oh, that sarcasm had returned "—can brace us, and pull us up if need be."

But Zed was already shaking his head. "I need to be at full strength to get us off this peak. It'll be harder going down than coming up."

At least he had explained that to Kyra more than once. The way the demiglider, and the air currents themselves, conspired to lift the demiglider up. When it needed to go down, it had to be piloted carefully, so the currents didn't shove it against the mountainside, destroying a wing—or worse, shattering and killing them.

Kyra nodded at him, mostly as an acknowledgement, a silent *I remember*. She didn't want to be as sarcastic as Uliana was, and Kyra was afraid she would be, if she wasn't careful.

"Do you think two people can handle this?" Kyra asked. She

gestured toward the bolts, for clarity. She meant the pulley system.

"If we send down our lightest two," Uliana said.

Kudos to her. Kyra would have expected Uliana to say that she absolutely had to go down. But Uliana was taller than many of the other climbers, certainly taller than Alyoshi.

As if reading her mind, Uliana said, "Matvei and I can handle the ropes and pulleys. We've done that system a million times. It'll help to have the bolts, but we won't rely on them."

Kyra breathed a sigh of relief. For a moment, she had truly thought the entire trip had been for nothing.

"However," Uliana repeated. "No exploring."

Kyra nodded, not sure how she had lost control of this entire trip. Maybe it was because her enthusiasm was so much greater than everyone else's. She had retreated into herself until she figured out these strange emotions.

"We don't have time for exploration anyway," Zed said. "If you're going to go down the mountainside today, you need to go as quickly as possible."

She turned toward him. He was watching the clouds.

"You think the weather will get worse?" she asked.

"It's not *if* the weather will get worse," he said. "It's when. So, yes, it'll get worse."

Kyra nodded. That was not a surprise, after their morning already.

"Let's set this up then," she said to Uliana. "We can reevaluate if we can't brace anything well enough."

"All right," Uliana said, and headed toward the back of the demiglider. Zed trailed after her.

Kyra put her hands on her hips, fighting her swirling emotions. She wanted to explore, but she wasn't even sure what they would be exploring.

For all she knew, that reflection point was a large area of shiny rock that caught the sun's rays every evening.

Even as she had that thought, though, she knew it was wrong.

Something about this whole place made her want to follow her hunches. Her training told her that hunches were dangerous —that she needed facts and data and detailed information.

But her heart, which had spoken to her from the beginning with Mount Vitaki, told her she had enough facts. She needed to experience it now.

And experience it she would.

THREE

They pounded three of the bolts in the middle of the area that Zed called the runway. It had the most wheel prints from his landings, and the least amount of dirt. It was also far away from the edges, so they wouldn't easily trigger any slides.

Matvei believed that pounding something into the dirt anywhere on top of this peak would start slides, but he had no facts to base that opinion on. He was also going by hunches, which made Kyra both annoyed and feel better. Because no one knew what was going on up here, everyone was reverting to behaviors she hadn't seen in a long time from these people, if ever.

And herself. She couldn't forget herself.

As they assembled the pulley system, which could be used with and without the bolts (if they broke off or got too wobbly), she made herself focus on the effort. Assembling a pulley was second nature to all of them. Each one of them had done so in the middle of an emergency, when another climber had been unable to pull themselves back up to the group.

The pulleys were designed to handle human weight, even

under the most difficult of circumstances, which Kyra hoped they would not experience here.

Zed made them promise that when they finished, they would pull the bolts from the ground, so that he had the full range of the mountain peak if the demiglider needed it.

Kyra had agreed. If she came back for a second time after her trip down the side of the mountain, she would make sure she had different equipment. The bolts and pulleys were built for the mountains, but they weren't the best system for a complex series of climbs. The systems that were the best were hugely expensive.

Once the pulley system was assembled, Kyra double-checked the ropes for breaks, cuts or burns. Then she inspected the levers and the flywheels. Last, she looked at the bolts. Those were the most mysterious part. They might've been weakened by the weather, but she couldn't tell just by eyeballing them.

Neither could anyone else, and they all checked.

The weather had gotten warmer as the sun became more intense. Warmer was a relative thing, though. Now, she didn't feel like her skin would seize up from the cold. Now, she was just chilly.

She knew that would disappear once she started down the mountain face.

Before they even started putting on their equipment, Kyra had given Alyoshi the chance to back out. He had been so negative all morning that she didn't want him to go if he was terrified. He wasn't that much lighter than Matvei or Uliana.

But Alyoshi insisted on going, and she had a hunch part of his reason was to keep an eye on her.

They tightened their clothes, then stepped into the special harness, with the ropes already in place. The belay tubes on both harnesses were made of mountainstone, as tradition required. Centuries of climbs and rappels had shown that belay tubes made from the actual mountains themselves gave the devices an additional, measurable strength.

Since Kyra was not an engineer, she had no idea why that was. But she had to trust them on this, as in all things.

Then she and Alyoshi double-checked their snacks and water containers. She hated the added weight, but there was no choice.

Then, with one final check, she and Alyoshi walked in tandem to the edge of the peak. He did not look down, and this time, neither did she.

They waited, though, just to see if the edge would hold their combined weight.

It did.

Kyra looked at Alyoshi. She didn't ask him if he was ready, like she usually would have. She didn't want him to back out of the trip.

She made a small circular gesture with her right index finger. Alyoshi sighed as he saw it, but followed the silent command.

He turned his back on the edge of the mountain.

So did Kyra.

The rest of her team stood near the bolts. Kyra had supervised setting up the ropes, anchoring them properly to the bolts, along with her favorite devices to feed the ropes through the openings in the bolts. But she was happy to have people back there, to take control should something go very wrong.

Uliana stood in the center, as if she expected to have to take charge. She probably would have to, given Zed's lack of experience with this part of the trip, and Matvei's surprising attitude problem.

But they looked as prepared as they could be.

"All right," Kyra said to Alyoshi. "Let's go."

His mouth moved. He said, "Yeah," but so softly that she couldn't really hear him. The wind teased his hair, but she couldn't feel any wind at all.

She pulled her ropes tightly, concentrating on her right hand —her brake hand—making sure that her gloves were thick enough to handle this should something go wrong.

Then she glanced over her shoulder at the edge, but managed not to look down.

The clouds were closer than they had been a moment before, almost like they were spotting her, or threatening to move in should she do anything wrong.

She leaned back in her harness, resting her butt against the equipment as if she was sitting on a chair. The last test, making sure it could handle her weight.

She hadn't been too concerned about it because she had double-checked everything. Her harness was good. So was Alyoshi's.

He mimicked her movement.

They hovered over the edge of the mountain, feet against the lip, for just a moment, before she began lowering.

She used her left hand—her guide hand—to ease herself down, feet against the mountainside. Her climbing shoes, designed to grip everything, had trouble finding purchase on the smooth surface, just like she expected.

That didn't stop her stomach from taking a small leap of its own. She usually didn't have nerves, but she had them this morning, because everything was unfamiliar, and it felt like the entire world was at stake.

She had to clear that expectation from her mind. The entire world was *not* at stake. If this didn't work, her life would not change.

But if it did work, as Magnus had predicted, then everything would be different.

She made herself concentrate on the descent. She leaned back slightly, keeping her toes against that smooth surface. Her legs were perpendicular to the mountain, the only part of this she really didn't have to think about.

That position was as natural as walking for her, because she had done it so often. And it was easier when the mountainside was smooth than when it jutted out at all angles.

Maybe that was the only benefit to this weird mountain—the predictable angle of its decline. She kept looking from side to side to make sure nothing was falling toward them or that she or Alyoshi had loosened something on the mountainside.

Alyoshi should have been doing the same, but he seemed to be having some trouble. He was only a few yards from her, but it seemed like he was on a different mountain altogether.

The muscles in his arms bulged. He was hanging on tightly. The wind kept moving his hair and, she realized, also trying to push him away from the mountain. When that didn't seem to work, it was trying to slam him into the mountain.

No wind bothered her at all, which was odd, because there were no natural barriers between them. He must have been rappelling down some kind of wind tunnel, some weird air current was catching him and avoiding her altogether.

As he moved his head, his gaze caught hers. She pointed up, knowing he wouldn't be able to hear her, even if she shouted.

But he should understand the gesture.

Did you want to go back?

She wasn't entirely, clear, though. She wasn't asking if *they* should go back. Just if *he* wanted to.

He shook his head, then glanced downward, as if searching for another place to place his feet. He almost never did that. Or maybe, he was just looking to see how far they had to go.

She wasn't going to let herself do that. She was going down bit by bit, measuring her pace the way she always did. She had learned to do so by counting the seconds between pushing back ever so slightly, and then moving forward.

Only she didn't really push back here. There wasn't much to measure against. It was easier—and better—to keep her feet on the mountainside, once she had found real purchase with her shoes.

Alyoshi was trying to push and pull himself, and it wasn't working. The wind was tangling his ropes, blowing his hair in his face, shoving him in different directions.

He had to hold tight to keep from slamming himself against the mountain.

She was about to tell him to go back up, when her feet hit air.

She looked down. What seemed like part of the rock face was actually a dark opening.

Then she looked up. She had gone faster than she expected to, maybe because she hadn't been fighting the geography of the mountainside.

She had reached the location of the reflection point.

She eased herself downward a little slower, because her feet were dangling now.

Alyoshi was near her, but he was swinging on his ropes, almost out of control in that wind. Now, it was blowing him backwards. Where her feet were dangling, his were being pushed underneath him, hurting his form.

She pointed up insistently with her guide hand, but he shook his head.

He clearly wasn't going to leave unless she did.

Besides, they appeared to have arrived.

She slid down farther on the rope, using more control than she had before because her feet were dangling. When her head finally cleared that lip, she blinked in surprise.

A cave greeted her.

Its top was as smooth as the side of the mountain. The top of the cave was an arch that extended as far as she could see.

She tried not to shift with excitement, but she had never felt this way—almost breathless with anticipation.

She wasn't sure what she had expected, but it hadn't been a cave.

She lowered just a bit more, to try to see deeper into the darkness, but she couldn't.

The air was still here, and smelled faintly perfumed, as if there was an unfamiliar incense burning inside.

She wanted to keep going, to see how far this went, but she was supposed to wait for Alyoshi. He was still struggling with that weird wind current, fighting his way down as if each drop was a victory.

He would be exhausted when they got ready to ascend. She would tell him to use the sign to encourage the team at the top to essentially pull him up.

She hoped he would listen.

She was dangling in the still air. She hated it. So she looked down, trying to see where the bottom of the cave opening was, to see if she could brace her feet on it.

As she twisted, she gasped with surprise. There wasn't a lip at the bottom of the cave opening. There was an entire platform —flat and perfect.

She could rest there, and wait for him.

She slowly eased down. The cave mouth was much larger than she expected—maybe thirty feet high and just as wide.

The interior of the cave was extremely dark, which also surprised her. She had thought, from down below, that perhaps there was something that would reflect the sun on this part of the mountain, a clear section or maybe just the angle of the mountainside.

She hadn't expected a cave. That seemed almost counterintuitive. There was nothing to reflect.

She glanced up. Alyoshi was struggling not to get tangled in his ropes, like a beginning climber. He wasn't even looking at her. He had to concentrate on what he was doing.

She eased the rest of the way down, then pushed away from

the edge, so that she wouldn't stop on that platform. If she and Alyoshi were working in tandem, one of them would have gone farther down while the other stopped on the platform.

But they weren't. He was still far above her.

So she checked first.

She didn't really go below the platform, but she went far enough that she could see what was underneath it. That way, she wouldn't have to change her configuration at all, from descent to ascent. Doing that would have taken more time than she wanted.

She kept her feet braced on the edge of the platform and peered over the side. The platform had been carved into the mountainside. The brown-black smoothness continued beneath the platform as if the cave didn't exist at all.

So, unless there was some kind of gaping hole underneath the platform that she couldn't see, the platform was secure.

She leaned forward even more and balanced on her toes, then pulled herself up just slightly. She shuffled her feet inward until they were flat on the platform, and then she stood, slowly, putting all her weight on her feet.

The platform shifted ever so slightly, making her gasp. Then a bright white light appeared inside the cave. Her heart pounded. She hadn't expected a light. Was that what the sun caught? Whatever caused the light?

Or was it a whoever? And if it was, how could it be a person? How would they have gotten here?

She looked up.

Alyoshi was clinging to his ropes with all of his strength, twisting in what looked like a gale, a gale she couldn't feel at all.

He had made it far enough down that she could reach him. She grabbed his ankles and stabilized him.

There was no wind. None. She had no idea why he was twisting like that.

He glanced down at her in surprise. He hadn't realized she was so close.

His entire body was trembling.

"How are you there?" he asked.

"There's a platform," she said.

"Where?" he asked.

His face was chapped and red. It certainly looked like he had windburn.

"Right beneath me," she said. She didn't ask why he wasn't seeing anything because she had no idea if the wind had covered his eyes in dust and debris. She'd had that experience. It was deeply unpleasant.

"I don't see it," he said, sounding almost panicked. Alyoshi never panicked. That was one of the things she liked most about him.

Yet this entire trip had put him on edge and had made him into someone she didn't recognize.

"Let me guide you," she said, gently pulling him downward, careful not to upset the delicate balance he had made with the ropes.

His body was trembling, a sign of just how much energy he had been using. She hoped he would have enough strength to make it all the way back to the top.

He scrabbled with his feet, as if they couldn't find the platform at all. She had to hold him in place to get his feet onto the platform, but he didn't seem to trust it.

Finally, he seemed to catch his balance. He stood, gingerly, but clung to his ropes as if he was afraid to let them go.

"What the hell is here?" he asked, blinking at her.

The light coming from inside the cave did not illuminate his face, which she found very strange. Every time she moved even slightly away from him, the wind started back up—at least around him—messing his hair, playing with the edges of his clothing.

"A cave," she said. "It goes really deep. And warm air is blowing out of the entrance."

"Where?" he asked.

"There," she said, trying not to sound as confused as she felt. "Where that light is coming from. Come closer, so you can feel the warmth."

"I don't see a light," he said.

She extended a hand, pointing into the cave itself.

"Okay, that's strange," he said. Then, gingerly, he extended his guide hand and it seemed to hit something solid. "This is just an indent in the rock. Not a cave."

"It's a cave." She put her hand next to his, but there was nothing solid near her fingers or her palm. Her hand went as far forward as it had before.

He looked at her with something like fright.

"This makes no sense, Kyra," he said. "Am I hallucinating?"

Or was she? It was a valid question, in the thin air.

"What do you see when you look at my hand?" she asked him.

"That it goes much farther forward than mine," he said. "But I'm hitting solid rock."

She threaded her fingers with his and then she extended their hands forward, past the point where his had gotten blocked.

"Okay," he said, still sounding scared. "I'm seeing our hands go through solid rock and disappearing."

Something was really wrong. He sounded convinced of what he saw, but it wasn't what was there.

She glanced up. The team was there, and he would need help getting back.

This climb was over, even though she didn't want it to be.

"Let me do one thing," she said. "Stay here, where it's warm."

He frowned at her—at least, she thought that was a frown. But she wasn't going to let it stop her.

This might be the only chance she ever got to see inside that cave.

50

She reached into her pack, and pulled out her spyglass. She put it to her eye, and peered as far from that light as she could.

But the light kept catching her. It came out of a vase, which sat on a table. It almost looked like the vase contained and controlled the light.

The table was long and clearly carved out of the mountainside. The table stood freely in the center of the cave's main room. Behind it, she thought she saw a fountain spewing water that reflected gold and white as the drops sailed through the air.

She turned away from the light, and blinked. It took a moment for her eyes to adjust. Then she saw shelves and tables in almost outlined against the darkness of the rest of the cave. The shelves and tables were covered with all kinds of devices—some she recognized, like compasses and telescopes and lanterns, but others she only had a vague sense of.

"Kyra." Alyoshi's voice trembled.

She had to take care of him. He was her top priority now. She would do so in a moment, but she just wanted to see as much as she could.

She swung the spyglass to the other side, and was surprised to see a harpsichord with a lute resting on its bench. Other instruments hung nearby—on the cave wall? On shelves? It was too dark to tell.

She saw the outlines of mandolins and crumhorns and natural horns and recorders. On one side were trumpets and bugles and circular horns. Beyond them, globes and maybe maps and perhaps still cameras like the ones that gave her fits in her work.

She wished she had them now, though. Even though it took forever to create and image, and even though the light was probably poor here, she would be able to prove to the others that this cave was worth exploring.

Kyra turned toward Alyoshi, and was about to hand him the

spyglass so he could confirm what she had seen when she actually looked at him.

Frost covered his eyebrows and eyelashes. His eyes were barely open, and he was shivering so badly that he looked like he would shake off his harness.

She wasn't even sure if he could see her anymore.

"Alyoshi!" she said. He blinked toward her. His hands looked frozen to his ropes, which was both good and bad. He wasn't falling backwards, but he wouldn't be able to help them pull him up.

Saving him was definitely on her now.

She reached into her kit and found more rope, tying him into the harness according to the protocol. Then she grabbed his guiding hand. It seemed to have frozen to his lead rope.

Her hands were frost-free. She wasn't even cold. The air coming from inside that cave was warming her.

But whenever she touched Alyoshi, she felt the chill of the wind—almost like a hint of wind, as if it were blowing through a badly sealed window.

She had been about to ask him if he could help with his ascent at all, when his eyes closed. That sent a stab of fear through her.

He didn't have a lot of time left.

She unhooked his braking hand so that it wouldn't get tangled in the ropes and attached him to the harness as best she could.

She would have to follow him up, using the procedure for unconscious climbers.

Before she alerted the others to pull him up, she used the climber's code, tugging the message for *unconscious climber*. Both Uliana and Matvei would know what to do.

Then she tugged three times on Alyoshi's ropes, and waited for a response.

She got it, along with an acknowledgment through her ropes that she would be handling the climb.

She let out a breath of air, marveling that she could see Alyoshi's breath, but not her own. It was as if she were indoors and he was out, even though there was nothing between them, no glass, no wall, no barrier of any kind.

The warm air from the cave enveloped her and protected her, kept her hands from shaking. The clouds still threatened off the sides of the mountain, but they seemed closer to Alyoshi than they were to her.

If only she could go inside the cave and wait. She could explore and see what all that equipment was. She could figure out the source of the warmth. She could—

Something tugged on her rope, catching her attention. It was a query.

Are you all right?

She must have waited too long between her communications.

Yes, she communicated in return. *One moment.*

There wasn't a lot of nuance in the climbing communications. She couldn't say that she still had to get Alyoshi ready or prepare herself. She couldn't apologize for lost time or try to explain the weird differences in the weather near the cave's mouth.

She couldn't think about any of that at the moment. She tucked Alyoshi's cold hands on his lap, made sure he was as stable as he could be, and then tugged the *lift* message on his rope.

It took a moment before she got an affirmative response on her ropes. By then, she had double-checked Alyoshi's position and double-checked her harness and ropes.

Unlike his, hers had no ice, no frost, and no problems. His looked like he'd been in deep snow. He was turning in the wind, the wind she couldn't feel, the wind that there was no evidence of on her side at all.

She couldn't think about that right now.

She eased herself over the side so she could assume the correct position—sitting in the harness, feet braced against the lip of the platform, legs perpendicular with the rock face—and then she sent the *lift me* tug.

That would activate everything—her rise alongside Alyoshi's. They would lift her a little slower than him, so that she would be slightly below him—but not on the same path. If he tumbled out of his harness—and people had—he would fall freely, without hitting her as he tumbled downward.

Her mouth went dry. She hadn't thought of all the things that could go wrong, not since she found the cave. The warmth no longer touched her and the light seemed to have faded, although it left a ghost of itself whenever she closed her eyes.

She was just beginning to wonder what was going wrong, why hadn't they started pulling Alyoshi upwards, when he started to move. His legs dangled freely and his head bobbed.

He was completely unconscious.

His harness rose maybe two feet higher than hers when the team up above started to lift her.

She could help. She had reset her belay tube so that it acted more like a pulley. She hadn't done that on Alyoshi's because to use the belay tube that way required the climber to be conscious and to know how to reverse the work they had done to get down.

Because she had the belay tube in place, her ascent was smoother than Alyoshi's. He bobbed and toppled from one side to another. The ropes jerked and more than once, she thought he was going to fall.

She couldn't catch him, but she could maneuver herself to prop him up if she had to.

She was hoping she wouldn't have to. She'd done that on

one climb, and it had been the most dangerous climb she had ever gone on. It had been a miracle that both of them survived.

Here, the distance wasn't as vast as that long-ago climb, but she still wasn't sure if Alyoshi was going to make it. The frost still coated his face and clothing. His legs dangled and his ropes still twisted.

Once he got well above the mouth of the cave, the winds seemed to die down. He still swung from side to side, but not as badly. The farther up he got, the less the wind seemed to be a factor.

As Kyra worked her way up, she didn't feel any wind at all. The air had gotten cooler, but that was only because that warm breeze from the inside of the cave had vanished.

She didn't understand what had happened on this trip. That would be something she would have to discuss with some scientists who specialized in wind or air currents or mountains. She had no idea what would cause one area of a mountainside to be completely calm, while a nearby section would be buffeted by severe winds, particularly when the mountainside was as smooth as this one was.

As she did half the work to pull herself up—figuring the team above had too much to do with Alyoshi—she focused on the wind and the science of air currents. She didn't want to think about what was happening with Alyoshi, nor did she want to think about what she had seen inside that cave.

It looked like strange treasure, a mishmash of things that she would never have placed together.

It implied that someone watched over the cave, kept an eye on it, maybe even used it.

But that implication might have been wrong, simply because what she saw made no real sense.

None of the items looked very old and yet some of them had to be. Many of them weren't being made any longer.

There was no obvious way for a person to get into the cave,

not without climbing down to it or up to it, so by rights, those items should have been covered with spiderwebs and dust.

Maybe someone lived there, deep inside the bowels of that cave. Maybe that was why warm air escaped. Maybe there was some kind of heating—a furnace of some kind, using rocks from the mountain itself to fire up parts of the furnace. Or oil or some other precious substance that would burn and keep an enclosed space like that warm.

But she didn't know, and she wanted to find out.

She let out a breath. She had promised herself she wouldn't think about any of that, and there she was, thinking about it, instead of paying attention to what was happening with Alyoshi.

He was tipped slightly backwards. One hand had fallen outside the ropes and dangled just like his feet.

If Alyoshi still had a long distance to go, Kyra would have hurried to catch up to him, sent a signal that she was moving closer to him, and take the risk of grabbing him and guiding him up.

But he was only about fifty feet from the top. Soon, she would see someone from her team leaning over and trying to ease him up.

And sure enough, just as she had that thought, Uliana's head peeked over the edge, concern on her face.

Kyra waved as a way of reassuring Uliana that Kyra was all right. And then she pointed at Alyoshi.

Uliana nodded, but didn't give Kyra any other acknowledgement.

If anything else, Uliana's expression grew even more grim. She pushed away from the edge, which surprised Kyra. Kyra had expected her to reach down and help Alyoshi make that last distance.

Kyra's heart started to pound. The situation seemed to be worse than she thought. She had no idea what was going on and she needed to.

Her feet were braced against the smooth side of the mountain. She had been pulling herself up slowly, without putting in as much effort from her legs as she could have.

Now she added them, pushing herself upwards even though she was beginning to feel fatigued.

Alyoshi dangled and twisted. His head lolled.

Zed peered over the edge, a deep frown on his face. Uliana appeared beside him. She was saying something to him, and he was nodding, but Kyra couldn't hear any of it.

They were laying on their stomachs, which gave them some leverage. Then Uliana looked at Kyra, and mimed *Stop*.

Finally what they were doing made sense. They were going to concentrate all of their efforts on getting Alyoshi to the top, and then they would worry about Kyra.

She nodded, and rested the toes of her boots against the mountain, hoping that would hold her enough.

Her upward movement had ceased. She wasn't happy with the position. She couldn't quite see what they were doing to get Alyoshi to the top. What she could see was a lot of movement— Uliana leaning, then disappearing, arms bracing, Zed turning slightly, Alyoshi spinning yet again.

Kyra's breath caught in her throat. Her team was so good at climbing and doing—well, most everything that it did—that she was no longer used to crises on important events.

She had known this would be hard. She just hadn't realized how dangerous it would be.

Waiting was not that good for her either. She hadn't realized how tired the ascent had made her. Her arms ached, and her feet were in an awkward position. There was still no wind here, but the clouds were getting closer.

Now, on top of everything else, she was worried about getting the demiglider off the mountain.

First things first, they had to get Alyoshi to safety. And then her.

Finally, Alyoshi's harness rose above the edge of the peak. Uliana and Zed dragged him toward them until Kyra could no longer see his legs or his boots.

He hadn't helped at all. She had held onto a small hope that he was injured or barely conscious and somehow able to assist with climbing over the edge. But he didn't. He had to be dragged.

She made herself release a small breath. She couldn't make up anything. It wouldn't help her.

Not that she was panicked. She wasn't. But she wasn't calm either. Things simply had not gone as planned.

She resisted the urge to glance over her shoulder, to look down at the cave opening. Perhaps that had been the most surprising thing of all. She was still drawn to it. She wanted to solve all of its mysteries—and part of her was deeply annoyed that Alyoshi had gotten hurt somehow. Because that would slow her down. She would have to deal with his injuries and the perceptions of danger those injuries would bring.

Then she raised her eyebrows, feeling odd. That last thought was not charitable of her. Was she that selfish that she worried more about what would happen because of Alyoshi's injuries than with the injuries themselves?

That didn't seem like her, and yet that was how she was feeling.

She made herself grip the ropes tighter, adjust her feet a little, and breathe the thin air. The morning had been surprising and upsetting. She needed to acknowledge that and move forward, whatever that meant.

She would think about the cave and its contents later. She would think about the future later. Right now, she had to get to the top of the mountain and get her team off of it.

At that thought, the signal came through her ropes. The team was going to help her the last of the way.

She adjusted her position one more time, then shot a glance

at the clouds. They looked even darker and thicker than they had before.

But sunlight covered her, almost like a halo of warmth. She was grateful for it.

She braced her toes, rose up ever so slightly, and leaned into the pull as the team above worked the ropes.

She didn't have far to go. And even though she felt every ache in every muscle while she waited, the wait had benefitted her. She had rested enough that she could put extra energy into getting to that mountain peak.

Or maybe her underlying worry fueled her. But she toed the smooth side of the mountain, used her arms as best she could, and finally her head rose above the lip.

She could see Matvei and Uliana, working the ropes. Zed wasn't visible at all, and neither was Alyoshi, although his harness lay on the ground like the abandoned skin of a snake.

Kyra pulled herself the rest of the way, until her feet found the top. She walked forward, still hunched, and slowly stood when she reached the area that seemed far enough away from that edge.

She used the flat of her hand to tell Matvei and Uliana to stop pulling on the ropes. The ropes fell beside Kyra's boots.

Her guide hand still held the ropes, but her brake hand cramped. Her back ached, and her shoulders were on fire from the effort.

The clouds seemed to have moved even closer to the edge of the mountain. Darkness surrounded everything except the peak itself.

Kyra undid her harness and stepped out of it. The air was colder here than it was on the mountainside, and now—finally —a breeze caressed her cheeks.

The sunlight was fading—not because it was late (it wasn't) but because the clouds were rolling in, like big waves of fog.

Uliana hurried toward her. Matvei was running toward the demiglider.

"Where's Alyoshi?" Kyra asked, when Uliana reached her side.

"Are you all right?" Uliana asked, ignoring her question.

"Exhausted, but all right," Kyra said.

"You're not cold?" Uliana asked. She seemed confused.

"There was a cave down there. I was on the platform. There was warm air coming from inside. I tried to get Alyoshi to the same place, but I couldn't. He never seemed to feel the warmth."

The words rushed out of Kyra. She had been more frightened than she realized.

"I don't understand," Uliana said.

"Neither do I," Kyra said, and as the words left her mouth, she realized just how little she did understand. Nothing made sense.

Matvei was coming back toward them. "We need to get out of here," he said. "Zed believes the weather won't hold."

Then Matvei peered at Kyra. "You're not covered in ice."

"No, I'm not," she said. "Something strange happened down there."

Matvei frowned at her, as if he didn't want to hear it. He seemed panicked, and, like Alyoshi, Matvei never panicked.

He moved past her and started disassembling the pulley. Uliana hurried to his side.

Kyra packed her equipment quickly, just like she had been trained to do in an emergency. She gathered it up, and tucked it under one arm, then walked to the two remaining members of her team. As she passed Alyoshi's harness, she grabbed it too, and dragged it toward the demiglider.

Matvei looked at it, then glanced at Uliana, as if asking her a question.

That simple look—and the only possible question it could

be (*do we need to have that weight in the demiglider?*) sent a chill through Kyra.

Her legs were wobbly, but she managed to reach Matvei and Uliana. They were beginning to disassemble the pulley.

"How is he?" Kyra asked.

"Not breathing," Matvei said and walked away.

The words felt like bits of ice, stabbing Kyra. Her gaze met Uliana's. Uliana's expression was carefully blank.

"Where is he?" Kyra asked.

"In the demiglider already," Uliana said.

Kyra shook her head, suddenly not sure she had understood Matvei. "Alyoshi will be all right then, right?" Kyra asked. "Once we get him below? Once we find a doctor?"

Uliana shook her head.

Kyra blinked, trying to understand. Maybe she did understand.

"He's...dead?"

Uliana nodded.

Kyra frowned, feeling unsettled. None of this seemed real. How could he be dead?

And then she remembered the set of his head as he lolled in his harness. Had she waited too long? What if she hadn't taken those few minutes to examine the interior of the cave with the spyglass?

Would Alyoshi have survived?

"I'd like to see him," she said quietly. Maybe then his death would seem real. Surely, she was having these odd thoughts because she didn't believe he was gone.

"He's in the demiglider already," Uliana said. "He's riding back with you."

Kyra almost asked if the others weren't coming back. She had trouble wrapping her mind around that—which was when she realized she wasn't thinking clearly at all.

Because of the thin air? Because she was just beginning to

feel grief? Because this entire trip had been strange and traumatic and not at all what she expected?

What Uliana meant became slowly became clear. Kyra was going to travel back with Alyoshi's corpse in the opposite seat.

Alyoshi's *corpse*.

Kyra pivoted and walked toward the demiglider. There was nothing else to say to the team anyway. She wasn't even sure how she could explain what had happened at the mouth of that cave.

She had never had a climb like that. She wasn't even sure she had had an experience like that in life in general—where the other person was so clearly having problems, so clearly suffering from something external, and those problems, that external thing, hadn't existed for her at all.

Her stomach was unsettled, her breath was uneven, and she was ever so slightly dizzy. She stopped, found the honey water inside her own pack, and made herself drink.

The water helped. The honey didn't lift her mood like it usually did, but it cut through her exhaustion. She knew from experience that the energy would not last, but it would at least get her through the next half hour or so.

She put the drink back into her side pack and walked the remaining distance to the demiglider. Zed was on the opposite side, checking the struts on the double wings.

Matvei was loading equipment into the small compartment on the back of the demiglider—and not doing so carefully. He was tossing items in, as if they were substitutions for his fists. He clearly wanted to punch something—or someone.

Kyra gave him a wide berth. She approached Zed instead.

His gaze was wary, and maybe filled with warning. She had the sense he didn't want to talk with her either.

"Where is he?" Kyra asked.

Zed swept a hand toward the middle of the demiglider. The bubble to that second section—the section she had ridden in—was open.

"Uliana said he's dead," Kyra said. She'd heard miracle stories about people who looked like they had frozen to death, only to have them thaw and revive.

She knew Zed had heard those stories too, and she respected him enough not to repeat them, as if she were questioning what he had just told her.

Zed must have seen all of that on her face. "Take a look for yourself."

She paused, then nodded. She had to use the struts and climb on the wing to get into the demiglider from this angle.

She held the struts gingerly, and put her feet carefully on the supported edges of the wings, like Zed had taught her long ago.

He stopped and watched her, a slight frown on his face. Was he wondering how she managed to move, given she had just completed a difficult climb? Or was he wondering why she was alive and Alyoshi wasn't?

Or both?

She reached the compartment easily. It would have taken very little for her to climb inside it, back into her seat.

He was leaning against the far side of the compartment, his legs resting at an unusual angle, one arm at his side and the other trapped beneath him. His head leaned on the edge of the compartment, his hair tangled around his face.

He looked like he was unconscious, not dead.

She climbed in the compartment after all, her movements shaking the demiglider. He didn't move at the disturbance.

She sat beside him and gently touched his arm.

His sleeve was damp, his hair matted. She reached for his face, so she could turn it toward her, just so she could see for herself what was going on.

His skin was like ice. It didn't even really feel like skin. It was too cold, and a little rubbery.

It took all of her strength to keep from recoiling. She turned his face toward her.

His eyes were open, which she hadn't expected, and clouded, as if something had covered them, dulling them. His skin was mottled red and white and black. Ice still coated his eyebrows. His lips were chapped and split, as if they had been too dry. Something had crusted around his nose—maybe blood, although whatever it was was awfully dark. The tip of the nose got frostbite first. Maybe that was the blackness she was seeing.

Her heart twisted. Alyoshi was dead. Very clearly, obviously, completely dead.

And he had been covered with ice. He had frostbite and maybe windburn, if the chapping on his cheeks was any indication. He had suffered on that climb, and she had been excited by what she saw, maybe even a tad warm in that strange light.

She had no idea what had happened to him.

Or maybe she should have been wondering what had happened to her.

She slowly released his face. Her fingers left tiny imprints on his skin. She had been grabbing him too tightly.

She took his shoulders, meaning to adjust his position, but his body wasn't moving much at all. It was too early for rigor mortis, wasn't it? Had he been that frozen?

Her stomach flopped, and she was suddenly queasy. She had to look away.

A million excuses ran through her head. She hadn't done this. He had opted to go with her. He had *insisted* on it. But he had wanted to go back before she did, and she had made him wait...

She pushed herself out of that compartment. She couldn't sit there any longer.

She climbed off the side of that demiglider to find herself alone. Zed was helping Matvei and Uliana disassemble the last of the equipment. The clouds had come even closer, and the wind was blowing as strongly as it had on that mountainside—against Alyoshi.

It was getting dark, even though it wasn't quite midday.

All of that had happened in the morning.

Kyra blinked, feeling tears, but they were getting blown about by the wind. She made her way to the others, and helped them with the last of the equipment.

The look Matvei gave her was colder than the wind. He gathered more equipment in his arms and walked away from her.

She had seen Matvei grieve a lost companion before. Matvei got angry first, because he didn't want to acknowledge the death.

She didn't blame him. She didn't want to acknowledge Alyoshi's death either.

She took pieces of the pulley and placed them in the bag that the team always carried. Zed took some of the longer pieces of equipment to the demiglider, and then, upon arrival, said something to Matvei.

Matvei made a fist, raised it above the demiglider, and Zed caught his hand. Then Matvei shook free, and walked away, heading toward the edge of the peak.

Kyra wanted to tell him not to go there, not with the wind coming up, not with the clouds moving in.

But she knew he wouldn't be able to hear her.

Uliana took a bag of equipment to the demiglider, where Zed was repacking what Matvei had placed in the back.

Kyra checked the ground to make sure nothing had fallen. Then she glanced at the sky. The light was almost gone.

She shivered. They had to leave, and soon.

She carried the bag she'd packed to the rear of the demiglider, and handed the bag to Zed. He nodded his receipt of it, but said nothing. Uliana left and walked toward Matvei.

Kyra hoped Uliana was going to tell him to come to the demiglider.

Kyra waited until Zed was done packing. Then she said, "Are we in trouble trying to get down?"

"It's not going to be pretty," he said, "especially with dead weight. I put Alyoshi in the center to balance, but really, he shouldn't be on the demiglider at all."

He said that pointedly, as if he expected her to give that order. She couldn't. She *wouldn't*.

"Can we make it down with him on board?" Kyra asked.

"I'm not sure we can make it down, period," Zed said.

Kyra's heart rate increased. "You said going down was easier."

"That day," he said. "That day I took you up, going down would have been easier. But the conditions were different, and this wind..."

He let the sentence trail off. She didn't need to hear the end of the sentence anyway. She knew what he meant.

"Do we have other choices?" she asked.

"I suppose we could camp," he said. "See if things are better tomorrow. But we don't have camping equipment and there's no real shelter if these clouds turn into the kind of storm I think they will. And if the wind gets any worse, the demiglider might not stay on the peak. We might lose our way down."

"I didn't expect this," she said.

His gaze measured her.

"I hadn't expected it either," he said.

Then he broke the gaze after a minute and walked to the front of the demiglider.

Uliana walked back to the demiglider, her hand on Matvei's back. His face was red, and he averted his eyes when he saw Kyra. She sighed inwardly, not exactly knowing how to traverse this complete change in her team, in herself, in everything.

She climbed back up on the side of the demiglider, and crawled into the compartment. She settled, like Zed had taught her the very first time, then put a hand on Alyoshi's damp sleeve.

He didn't notice. Of course, he didn't notice. But she willed him to understand.

"I'm so so sorry," she whispered. She could say nothing else. She was full of excuses and she needed to set them aside.

She had planned this trip and he had died on it. He was the first person who had ever died on a trip or something she had planned.

Other professors had lost team members, particularly when the professors were doing dangerous things. That was why no Students or Advanced Students were allowed on dangerous field missions.

There was even discussions about whether Practical Interns should have been allowed along. Although she hadn't had any here.

Thank goodness.

Because the uproar would be vast. Alyoshi was well-liked.

He was loved—by her too. He'd been a friend forever, and she hadn't listened to him.

Kyra leaned her head back, but kept her arm on his damp sleeve. She didn't want to let him go.

Zed stepped beside her and pushed the bubbleglass down. It clicked into place. He wasn't looking at her either, although his gaze rested on her hand for just a moment.

His expression softened, just a little, and then he moved behind her. She didn't turn, but the demiglider shook a little, as the bubbleglass covering Uliana and Matvei clicked into place.

They were ready to leave, except for Zed, who had to climb into the cockpit.

As he had done before their launch to the peak of Mount Vitaki, he walked around the demiglider, doing other things, things he said Kyra didn't need to know.

The clouds had circled the edge of the peak now, dark, almost black. A tiny ray of light pierced through them, and it felt like the light was illuminating her. The light covered her bubbleglass only, and warmed her.

She hadn't realized how cold she had become until that light touched her.

Zed climbed into the cockpit, the demiglider shaking under his weight. He adjusted the dials in front of him. That she did understand because he had explained it to her.

He was opening the wind vents on the windstone tube that ran beneath the demiglider. He needed power to get the demiglider off the mountaintop, and more power to let the demiglider plow through those clouds.

Otherwise, with the way the wind was blowing, the demiglider would slam into the mountainside.

Kyra swallowed hard. The demiglider still rocked in the wind. Occasionally a gust would buffet the demiglider and it would slide just a little.

Zed didn't seem to notice, although his hands worked faster than they had when the demiglider was landing.

His face wasn't showing any tension, but his entire body was.

Then he grabbed the stick with his right hand. With his left, he activated the speaker.

"Brace yourselves," he said. "This is going to be the ride of our lives."

The speaker clinked off. He slammed his left palm on one of the dials, and then with his right, pulled the stick to the right. The demiglider eased sideways.

Kyra's stomach fluttered, as if she was flying.

The demiglider turned all the way around, and she finally understood what Zed was doing.

He was putting the wind behind them—even though they were taking off from the opposite direction that they needed to go.

Kyra thought she heard Uliana's voice rise in the back—explaining what was going on to Matvei? Worrying about what Zed was doing? Trying to get Zed's attention?

Kyra didn't know, and there was no way to know. She couldn't make out what Uliana was saying. Zed probably hadn't even heard the faint voice.

As the demiglider rocked in the wind, Alyoshi's body slipped a little.

Now, instead of holding it as comfort, or support, or in memory, Kyra was bracing it, just a little.

Maybe she should have grabbed Alyoshi's arm when they were descending or when they were at the cave's mouth. Would that have changed anything? Would he still be alive?

She shook her head, trying to get those thoughts out of her mind. But it wasn't working, particularly since that ray of golden light still attached itself to her, even as the demiglider moved into different positions.

The floor was vibrating under her feet. Zed had explained that, saying that as the demiglider's windstone tube filled with air, the stored power would make the demiglider seem almost alive.

Of course, with the wind and the encroaching clouds, the movement and the whistle that echoed over the windglass, everything seemed alive at the moment.

Everything except Alyoshi.

The floor's vibration became a shaking and the shaking nearly rattled her teeth out of her head.

Then, when she thought she couldn't take anymore, the demiglider launched itself forward, wheels on the ground, heading into the clouds.

She felt the lift. There was a difference. No rattling, no vibration, just a sudden smoothness as the demiglider caught some kind of current.

The clouds parted in front of them, unlike when they arrived, but the parting wasn't 100 percent. The side of the demiglider with Alyoshi was dark, and rain pelted the windglass, but on her side, the golden sunlight continued, as if they were flying under perfect blue skies.

If only she could lean forward or climb from one compartment to another, so that she could sit by Zed. His compartment was a single-person compartment, and it was half in sunlight and half in rain and clouds.

He didn't seem to notice, though, or if he did, he wasn't letting on. His hands were moving even faster, although a moment ago she would not have thought that possible. He didn't say a word—not that she could hear him—but something in his posture was different.

If she had to guess, she would have thought him panicked. But the Zed she knew didn't panic—about anything.

The demiglider seemed to float upward, but she had no real way of measuring what was happening. The light reflected off her clothing, but Alyoshi was in darkness—except where her hand was touching him.

She peered over her shoulder. The clouds had formed around the back of the demiglider. Only the area where she sat was 100 percent in the light.

Uliana's cool gaze met hers. Uliana frowned slightly, as if to acknowledge that she was seeing the changes in the light.

Matvei watched Kyra turn around, but the moment she looked at him, he looked away.

She nodded once, then turned back.

The area in front of the demiglider was covered in clouds.

Zed was flying forward without any visibility at all.

But the demiglider seemed to be moving quicker. And it felt sturdier than it had on the ride here.

He was pushing the stick and if Kyra squinted, she could see that the nose was pointed straight forward.

At some point, he would have to point that nose downward. They were in a valley, but there were a lot of peaks near Mount Vitaki. One wrong turn and they'd fly right into one.

Kyra took a deep breath and willed this flight to go smoothly. None of them needed more trouble.

As if it heard her thought, the demiglider banked sharply to the right. Zed used both hands to grab the stick, but it seemed to be moving on its own.

Then the demiglider veered upwards, and as it did, Kyra saw mountains on her side. If the demiglider hadn't veered, hadn't banked, it would have crashed into them.

Zed had his hands in the air. The stick seemed to be moving on its own.

He glanced over his shoulder at Kyra, and his eyes were wide. Frightened.

Fear gripped her. He wasn't flying the demiglider. He was letting her know that it was out of his control.

She waved a hand at him, as if to say, *Do your job!*

He shrugged and extended his hands even more, as if he couldn't do the job at all.

He mimed reaching for the stick, but as he did so, the top seemed to bend away from him, while the middle of the stick didn't bend at all.

Surely, that was an illusion of the light. Sticks did not move like that.

The nose of the demiglider turned downward, and the rest of the demiglider followed, going much faster than Kyra would have liked.

Zed wasn't even trying to guide the demiglider. He was hanging onto his seat with both hands. The muscles in his neck stood out, as if he was clamping down on his jaw.

Kyra didn't know if Uliana and Matvei could see Zed. Kyra hoped they couldn't, because just looking at him was making her more terrified than she had been on that mountainside, before she realized what was going on with Alyoshi.

She wished she could convince herself that what Zed was doing was a normal part of flying the demiglider, but she knew it wasn't. She had asked him on that very first flight why he had the stick, what the dials meant, and why he was there.

Gliders float on air currents, he said. *You have little control of them. But this glider is a* demi*glider for a reason. It needs its pilot. It's too heavy to fly just on air currents. It has a propulsion system. It can and should be steered. It's just not something you hope will make its way down safely.*

She raised her gaze to him now. He was leaning forward, as if he was watching the dials, which had iced over. There was ice in the cockpit? She wasn't cold.

But Alyoshi was. She had just attributed that to the fact that his body was no longer producing any warmth.

If this demiglider goes down, she thought as clearly as if she had spoken the words, *I will die.*

The light expanded suddenly and engulfed the entire demiglider. The clouds receded somewhat, and the ice on the dials melted, leaving beads of water on the front.

Zed reached out cautiously and wiped off the water with his fingers. Then he grabbed the stick with one hand.

The stick seemed to respond this time.

He visibly let out a breath, then moved the stick. The demiglider continued its downward path.

As the clouds burned off, Kyra realized the demiglider was in the very center of the valley, following the river below. They were off course if they were heading back to the plateau they had taken off from, but there were plenty of places to land near the river.

She let out a breath, finally able to acknowledge just how terrified she had been.

Her fingers were wrapped in the fabric of Alyoshi's sleeve, as if she had been leaning on him to give her comfort.

She glanced at him one final time: she had always leaned on him for comfort. Tears threatened for the first time. How had she ignored him? How had she made that mistake? What was *wrong* with her?

She didn't really feel like herself. Was it finally figuring out what was causing the reflection off Mount Vitaki? Or was it that cave? Or was it some kind of reaction to the grief?

She didn't know, and she wasn't quite ready to unpack it yet.

Sunlight covered the entire valley. The flowing brown water of the river gleamed and winked at her, as if they both understood some kind of secret.

She twisted in her seat. The horrid dark clouds had taken over the entire top of Mount Vitaki. She couldn't see it at all anymore. And yet, as she looked at it, she wanted to.

Part of her was ready to head back up to the top right now.

And that wasn't like her at all.

She made herself look down, made herself look at the dials.

Zed still clung to the bottom of his seat. The dials still had moisture on the side, and the stick was holding steady, seemingly by itself.

She shuddered just a little. Maybe she was dying. Maybe she had passed out on that trip down the mountainside, and she was hallucinating all of this.

That made as much sense as what she was seeing.

The stick turned, and then the demiglider turned. It continued downward, away from Mount Vitaki.

She unhooked her fingers from Alyoshi's sleeve. Her hand was wet. She wiped it on her pants, feeling just a little ill.

The demiglider was traveling silently. The wind didn't even whistle around it, like it had up above. And the demiglider wasn't moving around like it had. It stayed stable, as if whatever propelled it kept it steady too.

Finally, the demiglider settled just above the river. If it went much farther, it would land in the water.

Zed picked up his right hand, squeezed it as if he had hurt it by clinging so hard, and gingerly placed it on the stick. Then he wiped the dials again with his left thumb.

Now, the stick was responding to his touch. He took the demiglider to a new height, moved it slightly away from the river, and slowly turned it around.

Even though she hadn't consulted with him, she knew what he was doing. He was heading back to the plateau they'd launched from, not far from her adobe home, not far from the buildings where she taught students from the academy how to be archeologists.

The very thought—the word "archeologist," actually—made her stomach jump with anticipation, and as she acknowledged that, an image of all of those items from the cave rose in her mind.

How had they gotten there? Was there an entrance on the ground that she and her students had missed? That everyone had missed? Should she check for it? Should she send some kind of team to find it all?

Then she shook herself, trying to get the thoughts from her head. They were easier to think about than what she would say when the team arrived back at her compound, with Alyoshi dead.

She made herself look outside the demiglider, at the blue sky and the mountain platform that was just ahead—or seemed to be just ahead. She couldn't really judge distance in this kind of light.

Zed wasn't moving as quickly as he had before, but that hunch in his shoulders, the way he leaned forward...he still seemed panicked to her.

Why wasn't she panicked? Was she numb?

She didn't turn around any longer. Instead, she watched as the ground got closer and closer, and finally, the demiglider bounced along it.

A handful of Practical Interns came out of nearby buildings, smiling and waving, and oh, she didn't want to deal with them.

She should have thought about how to talk to them, about what to do. That was her job, not Uliana's or Zed's or Matvei's.

Magnus was with the Practical Interns. Had he brought them to help himself through the long wait?

She wrenched her brain away from that cave, the reflection point, the mountain, and made herself focus on the next few hours.

She had to decide what to do. She had to figure out how to handle this.

And she had to talk to Alyoshi's family.

She didn't have time to contemplate the cave, even though that was all she really wanted to do.

FOUR

S omehow, they got the demiglider unloaded. Somehow, she told everyone—in halting language—that Alyoshi had died up there. The moment went from celebratory to funereal in an instant.

It didn't help that she couldn't explain what happened— why he froze to death and she hadn't been cold at all. She mentioned the cave, the items in it, but no one seemed excited about that. Everyone who listened, except maybe Uliana, seemed surprised that Kyra would talk about the inside of that cave at all.

Kyra had no idea how to thread the emotions. She had no way to know what was normal and what wasn't. Her legs wobbled. She was so tired.

Magnus took her arm and led her to a nearby rock. Then he went back to the Practical Interns and talked with them, gesturing, getting them to unpack the demiglider, and deal with Alyoshi's corpse.

Or maybe Magnus had dealt with it.

Kyra didn't watch. She'd worry about all of that a little later. After she sat for a moment and caught her breath.

She found herself looking at Mount Vitaki.

The legends said that there was magic on that mountain. The legends said that only a handful of people belonged anywhere near it. The legends said that evil could come from that mountain and attack anyone at any time.

She hadn't believed any of it. She wasn't sure she believed the magic part now, but she understood the sense of evil. Whatever happened to Alyoshi—that had been awful and it had seemed personal against him.

The mountain wanted her. It hadn't wanted him at all.

She understood that now. She wished she had understood it while she was on the mountainside, but something had clouded her brain. That desire, which she still felt. That need to get inside that cave, to be near that mountain, to figure out exactly what was going on.

She felt more clearheaded now, but she wasn't sure why.

One thing she was sure of: she would be disciplined by Serebro Academy. She might not be able to bring Practical Interns up here again.

She might be called back.

She couldn't be called back.

If the academy demanded that she leave the Razbitay Mountains, she would resign.

Maybe she would resign anyway.

Eventually, the activity settled down. Magnus found his way to her side. He had two mugs of peppermint tea. Of course he had two mugs of peppermint tea.

"There will be a disciplinary hearing," he said quietly, as he handed her a mug. She took it, startled at the warmth.

The steam smelled good. Her stomach growled. She hadn't realized she was hungry. She didn't know how long it had been since she ate.

He sat down beside her. She had to scoot over to make room for him on the rock.

"If you go back," he said.

"What?" she asked, before she put the sentences together in her head. *There will be a disciplinary hearing, if you go back.* "Why wouldn't I go back?"

Magnus gave her a sideways smile.

"If you resign and back date it," he said, "you own this discovery, not the academy."

He was being mercenary. At a time like this. She wasn't sure why.

She blinked at him, confused.

"You can't be disciplined then," Magnus said. "And maybe you shouldn't be disciplined anyway. Alyoshi went with you as a friend. He's not part of the archeology department."

Present tense. Part of Magnus was thinking clearly and the other part was not.

"And Uliana and Matvei are locals now," Magnus said. "We'll pay them, you and I. Not the academy."

Kyra frowned at him.

"You found things, right?" Magnus asked. "That's what you said. You found things in that cave."

"Saw things," she said.

A lot of things. Things that didn't belong there, in a cave midway up a mountain.

"That might be true," she said. "Why is that important?"

It was important to her, of course. But everything was clouded by Alyoshi's death. The academy would certainly see it that way.

"Because we are at the crossroads of two futures, you and I," Magnus said. "If we go back to Serebro right now, our lives will get picked over. You'll be disciplined, and maybe even lose your sinecure. You won't be working with Practical Interns, not after a death like this. Your life will never be the same. *Our* lives will never be the same."

"They won't be anyway," she said.

"That's right," Magnus said. "If we stay, we can control our own future. Maybe even figure out what you discovered."

"You have a hunch," she said.

He nodded. "Remember that legend? The one about the warriors on the mountain?"

She blinked. She had forgotten it, thinking it silly. That warriors had come through a hole in the Razbitay Mountains and nearly destroyed this part of Dorovich. Centuries ago. Maybe even a thousand years ago.

Long before the Qavnerian Protectorate existed. Before anyone wrote things down. Some of the locals liked retailing the legend, but others would shush them, as if the legend was unspeakable.

Maybe it was. The legend had the stuff of myth—warriors descending. Half-humans half birds attacking. Creatures never before seen taking over entire villages.

She had always assumed that was one of the reasons the valley was forbidden—because some thought the mountain dangerous, and others thought the purveyors of this legend crazy.

The danger and the crazy had left centuries ago. The warriors disappeared as if they had never been, and the stories were simply that. Stories to scare children, to keep them away from one of the more dangerous places on the continent.

"What about that legend?" she asked.

"What if the warriors did come out of the mountain?" Magnus asked. "Through that cave. As a surprise."

"There was no way out of that cave," she said, and immediately knew she was wrong. There was. They could have rappelled all the way down to the valley floor from that plateau.

Which begged the question: how had the warriors gotten in the cave in the first place?

Her heart lifted and as it did, her brain told her she was betraying Alyoshi.

80

But she wasn't. If she found answers, then maybe she would make his death worthwhile, right? That had been the whole point. To learn what was going on in this little corner of Dorovich.

"Have you done the numbers?" she asked.

Magnus nodded. "I kept getting two sets for today, and they didn't make sense until you returned. Now they do."

She waited. She still hadn't sipped the tea, but the peppermint scent *was* soothing, a thought that made her smile just a little ruefully.

"If we go back to the academy," he said, "we have a dark future."

"And if we stay?" she asked.

"Then your mission to the mountain truly was auspicious. The Kirilli name will reverberate through the entire history of Dorovich for decades to come."

She had no idea how he knew that. For all she knew, he was making it up. But after the crazy things she had seen today, she was much more willing to believe in his predictions than she had been at any other point in their lives.

Or maybe she just wanted to believe to avoid the discipline that she would face if she left the mountains.

It really wasn't a decision at all.

"All right," she said quietly. "We'll stay."

Magnus hugged her with one arm, pulling her close. Then he let her go, and she felt the loss of him, almost more than she felt the loss of Alyoshi.

"I'll take care of everything," Magnus said. "You just focus on that mountain."

She nodded, then turned slightly on the rock. The sun was setting. A bright white light beamed out of the side of Mount Vitaki and coated her in brilliance.

No one else was touched by the light. No one else even seemed to notice.

It was almost as if the mountain was winking at her, telling her that it too approved of the decision.

She nodded once, in a kind of mental acknowledgement, and then turned away.

Even though Magnus said he would handle everything, there were things only she could do. Interactions with the mountain, decisions to be made here in the valley.

She would do all of that.

And she would never go back to Serebro.

Somehow, that thought didn't break her heart.

She wondered, now, if anything ever could.

THE SACRIFICE

BOOK ONE OF THE FEY

KRISTINE KATHRYN RUSCH

NEW YORK TIMES BESTSELLING AUTHOR

If you enjoyed *The Reflection on Mount Vitaki*, you may enjoy
the entire Fey Saga! What follows is a sample chapter from book
one in the series, *The Sacrifice: The First Book of The Fey*.

THE VISION

T HE LITTLE GIRL slammed into Jewel at full run, then slid and fell on the wet cobblestone. The girl sat for a moment, her skirts wrapped around her thighs, revealing the pants-like undergarments the Nyeians insisted on trussing their children in. Jewel hadn't moved. Her hip ached from the impact of the girl's body, but Jewel didn't let the pain show.

She hadn't expected to see a child on the narrow, dark streets of the merchant center of Nye's largest city. The stone buildings towered around the cobblestone road. Even though the sun had appeared after a furious thunderstorm, the streets were just as dark as they had been during the sudden downpour.

"Esmerelda!" A woman's voice, sharp and piercing, echoed on the street. The passersby didn't seem to notice. They continued about their business, clutching their strange round timepieces as they hurried to their destinations.

The little girl tugged on her ripped skirts and tried to stand. Jewel recognized the look of panic on the child's face. Jewel had felt that herself in the face of her grandfather's wrath. Jewel took two steps toward the girl and crouched, thankful that she was wearing breeches and boots that allowed such freedom of movement.

"Why were you running?" Jewel asked in Nyeian.

"Felt like it," the girl said.

Good answer. Nyeian children didn't play enough. Their parents didn't allow it. The girl had courage.

Jewel extended her hand. The girl stared at it. Jewel's slender fingers and dark skin marked her as Fey, even more than her upswept eyebrows, black hair, and slightly pointed ears.

"Esmerelda!" The woman's voice had an edge of panic.

"She won't like your being dirty," Jewel said.

The little girl's lower lip trembled. She reached for Jewel's hand when a screech resounded behind them. Jewel turned in time to see a woman wearing a dress so tightly corseted it made her appear flat swing an umbrella as if it were a sword. Jewel stood and grabbed the umbrella by its tip, pulling it from the woman's hand.

"You were about to hit me?" Jewel asked, keeping her tone level but filled with menace.

The woman was a few years older than Jewel, but already her pasty skin had frown lines marring her eyes and mouth. Her pale-brown eyes took in the thin vest that Jewel wore in deference to the heat. "What were you doing to my child?"

"Helping her up. Have you an objection to that?"

The woman glanced at her child. Jewel stood between them. Then the woman bowed her head. Her brown hair had touches of gray.

"Forgive me," she said, not at all contrite. "I forgot myself."

"Indeed." Jewel put the tip of the umbrella on the cobblestone and leaned her weight on it. Sturdy thing. It would have made a good weapon, and she had no doubt the woman had used it as such during the recent conflict. "Forget yourself again, and your daughter may lose her mother."

"Is that a threat, mistress?" The woman brought her head up, eyes flashing.

"Mistress." Nyeian term of respect. The Fey did not believe in such linguistic tricks. There were other ways of keeping inferiors in line.

"You're not important enough to threaten, my dear," Jewel said, using the linguistic trick to her own benefit. "I was merely warning you. As a kindness."

She knelt beside the little girl again.

The girl's eyes were tearstained. "Don't hurt my mommy," she whispered. "I didn't mean to bump you."

"I know," Jewel said. She adjusted the girl's heavy skirts and helped her to her feet. Then she handed her the umbrella. It was almost as tall as the child. "You just remind your mother that we are no longer your enemies. You have to learn to live with us now."

The mother watched Jewel's every movement. Jewel brushed the dirt off the child's skirts, marveling at the thickness of the fabric. Jewel would suffocate in clothing like that.

"You might also want to let your mother know that pants are more practical for children, male or female."

"I thought you weren't going to change our customs." The woman spoke again, her tone full of bitterness, even though she bowed her head again in the submissive gesture the Fey had commanded. Jewel thought of challenging her on her rudeness but decided the battle wasn't worth her time. She was already late for the meeting with her father.

"We change only the customs that interfere with healthy, productive living. Children are born to move, not mince like some expensive creature at a Nye banquet." Jewel smiled and reached a hand under the woman's chin, bringing her head up so that their gazes met. "She wouldn't have run into me if she had been dressed properly."

"You have no right to change how we live," the woman said.

"We have every right," Jewel said. "We choose to allow you your customs because they keep you productive. You are the one without rights. You lost them six months ago when my grandfather became the leader of Nye."

Finally the panic that had been missing from the woman's face appeared. Her round eyes narrowed and her mouth opened just a bit. "You're the Black King's granddaughter?"

Jewel let her hand fall and resisted the urge to wipe her fingertips on her breeches. "Aren't you lucky I was in a good mood this morning? Threatening me is like threatening all of the Fey at once."

The woman's face flushed with terror. She grabbed the little girl and pulled her close. Jewel ignored the gesture. She took a loose strand of the little girl's brown hair and tucked it behind the girl's ear.

"Take good care of your mother, Esmerelda," Jewel said, and continued down the street.

At the corner she glanced back, saw the woman still standing in place, the little girl clutched against her side. Jewel shook her head. The bitterness would get the Nyeians nowhere. They were part of the Fey Empire now. The sooner they all realized it, the better off they would be.

Jewel clasped her hands behind her back. The air was warm and muggy after the storm, except in the shadows of the great buildings. Her grandfather had taken the greatest, the Bank of Nye, and made it his own. Four stories of stone standing like a palace in the merchant section, the building was the closest thing to a palace that the Nyeians had ever made.

The streets were nearly empty for midday. The half-dozen Nyeians gave Jewel a wide berth as they passed her on the street. The Fey guards standing in front of each Fey-occupied building nodded to her as she passed. She nodded in return.

Six months since the Nyeians surrendered, and still her

grandfather felt the need for guards. Six months without fighting, and she was growing restless.

Like her father.

He had a plan for the next battle. She was ready, even though her grandfather wasn't sure if the entire force was ready to move again. Her brothers didn't think so, but they were young. The last year of the Nye campaign had been the first time any of the boys had seen battle.

Jewel had fought since she was eleven—nearly seven years—and she had never progressed beyond the Infantry, much to her father's and grandfather's dismay. Her brothers were delighted. They all assumed that her lack of Vision would mean that she would be passed over as heir to her grandfather's throne.

She hadn't told any of them about her strange dreams. She hadn't even visited the Shaman about them.

Finally Jewel arrived at the Bank of Nye. It stood in the center of a cobblestone interchange. Sunlight touched a small corner of the stone, causing it to heat, and steam to rise from the wet. Through an open window she could hear her father's voice mingling with her grandfather's.

They were fighting, just like she knew they would be.

Every time her father mentioned moving beyond Nye, leaving the Galinas continent and heading out to sea, her grandfather objected. The next place to conquer was an island in the middle of the Infrin Sea. Blue Isle had been a major trading partner with Nye. It had also done some business with countries on Leut, the continent to the south. Blue Isle was a gateway that Nye could never be. But it was a gateway that the Black King believed the Fey were not ready to use.

Jewel knew better than to interrupt an argument between her father and her grandfather. Her father had asked her to wait for him, and wait she would. Outside.

Jewel sat on the flagstone steps and propped one booted foot against the wall across from her. She leaned against the cool stone walls, not caring that the roughness of the stone pulled strands of hair from her braid. This was as close as she could get to the open window, but even if she closed her eyes and concentrated, she could not make out the words.

No one else realized the importance of the battle within. Nyeians scurried by, moving as quickly as people could in six layers of clothing, their round faces red and covered with sweat. Jewel had often joked that the Nyeians had lost the war because they didn't know when to take their clothes off.

Not that the wars had hurt business in Nye. The shops were open, and the street vendors hawked wares as if nothing had happened. Fortunately, the bank was on a street filled with other austere stone buildings, a street where no vendors were allowed. She wouldn't have been able to hear anything at all if the vendors had been camped on the cobblestone.

The Nyeians ducked in and out of shops without once glancing at the open gaily colored flags outside. The flags indicated the type of merchandise—blue for items made in Nye, yellow, green, red, and purple for items made in other countries. The Bank of Nye had transferred its business to the brick building directly across the street, and more than one trader had entered, a money pouch clutched tightly to his hip.

Jewel closed her eyes and a wave of dizziness hit her. The world tilted, and she suddenly felt great searing pain burning into her forehead. Her father shouted, "You've killed her!" and a voice answered in a tongue she did not recognize. Then her father shouted, "Someone help her! Please help her!"

Her breath came in ragged gasps. She opened her eyes. A man leaned over her, his eyebrows straight, his hair long and blond. His features were square. He was neither Fey nor Nyeian. His skin was pale without being pasty. He had a rugged, healthy look she had seen only in the Fey, but his features were stronger, as if drawn with a heavy hand. He spoke to her in that strange tongue. *Orma lii,* he said, then repeated a different word over and over.

He cradled her in his arms, holding her with a tenderness she had never felt before. Then the scene shifted. The strange man still held her, but she wore her father's healing cloak.

A Healer slapped a poultice on her forehead. It smelled of redwort and garlic, and stopped the burning from spreading. "She'll live," the Healer said, "but I can promise no more."

"What did she say?" the strange man asked. His Fey had an odd accent.

"That she'll live," her father replied. He was speaking Nyeian. "And maybe little more."

The strange man pressed her closer. "Jewel." He kissed her softly. "*Ne sneto. Ne sneto.*"

She reached up and touched him with a shaking hand. This night was not how she'd dreamed it would be.

Then the world shifted back. She had moved down two steps, and her forehead tingled with remembered pain. Her throat was dry. A Vision. A real Vision, powerful enough to make her lose her place in the present.

Her heart was pounding rapidly against her chest. She had never heard her father sound so terrified. Nor had she ever seen anyone like that man. His pale skin, straight eyebrows, and blue eyes marked him as not Fey, and his square features and appearance of health meant he wasn't Nyeian. Yet he knew her well enough to cradle her with love.

The bank door slammed open and her father stormed out, his black cloak swirling around his legs. He was among the tallest Fey, and he usually used that height to great effect. Now, though, he seemed even taller than usual.

Jewel had never seen him this angry outside of battle.

She made herself swallow, wishing she had something to ease her sudden thirst. Then she got up slowly, afraid the dizziness from the Vision would return.

"So he said no, huh?" she asked. She had to look up to see his face.

"He said yes." Her father bit out the words as if he resented them.

She frowned. "Then why are you angry? You want to conquer Blue Isle."

Her father looked at her. His eyebrows swept up to his hairline, his eyes fierce. "Because he said I am making a mistake. That I am fighting because I am addicted to slaughter, not because I want to add to the Empire. He said it would be good for me to die on the battlefield so that I don't bring that taste for death to the chair of the Black King."

Harsh words. Too harsh. The fight between the men must have been deep. "He was speaking in anger," she said.

"He believed it was truth." Her father stomped down four stairs, then stopped. At this vantage she was as tall as he was. "No matter what he says, I am taking you with me."

"What about my brothers?" Jewel asked. The last time her father had taken her on a campaign, he had done so that she might care for the boys.

"They're too young for this trip. Meet me in my quarters tonight and bring the Warders. We have a campaign to plan."

He turned his back on her and continued down the stairs. When he reached the street, the Nyeians backed away from him. He hurried across the cobblestone, his cloak fluttering behind him.

Jewel braced one hand against the wall. The dizziness was gone, but a disquiet had settled into the pit of her stomach. She had had her Vision after her father had decided to go to Blue Isle. Were the two connected?

She shook her head. She knew better than to make such speculation about Visions. They existed to guide leaders. She should have been happy she had a Vision of such strength. It settled a fear that she would never have the power to be Black Queen.

In spite of herself she felt an odd joy. Her father would take her on her first real campaign—not as a soldier and caretaker for children, but as a leader. One who would help plan.

No matter what her grandfather said about settling, he was wrong about one thing: the fight was in their blood. The restlessness she had felt for the last six months would be put to good use.

She pushed herself away from the clammy stone wall. The face from her Vision rose in her memory.

"Orma lii," she whispered, even though she didn't know what it meant. She was going to face her destiny as a Fey should, in full battle gear, weapons drawn.

Follow Kris on BookBub!

I value honest feedback, and would love to hear your opinion in a review, if you're so inclined, on your favorite book retailer's site.

Be the first to know!

Just sign up for the Kristine Kathryn Rusch newsletter, and keep up with the latest news, releases and so much more—even the occasional giveaway.

So, what are you waiting for? To sign up go to kristinekathrynrusch.com.

But wait! There's more. Sign up for the WMG Publishing newsletter, too, and get the latest news and releases from all of the WMG authors and lines, including Kristine Grayson, Kris Nelscott, Dean Wesley Smith, *Pulphouse Fiction Magazine, Smith's Monthly,* and so much more.

To sign up go to wmgpublishing.com.

ABOUT THE AUTHOR

International bestseller Kristine Kathryn Rusch wrote seven books featuring the Fey before traditional publishing issues in the United States stymied her. The extremely popular series became a bestseller in multiple languages, including French, Italian, German, Polish, and Czech. When the first book, *The Sacrifice,* first appeared in the United States, it was hailed as one of the best fantasy novels of the year. Rusch took an unintended twenty-plus year hiatus from the Fey after completing the second full mini-saga. Spurred by a successful Kickstarter for a novella featuring the Fey, she dove back into the project. She explains her journey back to the Fey in *Lessons from the Writing of The Fey*. All seven of the books are back in print through WMG Publishing, and have garnered new readers worldwide. Rusch recently published the novella, *The Reflection on Mount Vitaki*, and has completed two new novels, with a third underway.

Rusch writes in many genres, from science fiction to mystery, from western to romance. She has written under a pile of pen names, but most of her work appears as Kristine Kathryn Rusch. Her Kris Nelscott pen name has won or been nominated for most of the awards in the mystery genre, and her Kristine Grayson pen name became a bestseller in romance. Her science fiction novels set in the bestselling Diving Universe have won dozens of awards and are in development for a major TV show. She also writes the Retrieval Artist sf series and several major series that mostly appear as short fiction.

Rusch broke a number of barriers in the sf/f field, including being the first female editor of *The Magazine of Fantasy &*

Science Fiction. She has owned two different publishing companies, and she is an in-demand speaker about business and craft. She also writes a highly regarded weekly publishing industry blog. Find out more about her work at kriswrites.com, and more about the Fey at thefeyseries.com.

facebook.com/kristinekathrynruschwriter

patreon.com/kristinekathrynrusch

bookbub.com/authors/kristine-kathryn-rusch

THE FEY SERIES
BY KRISTINE KATHRYN RUSCH